CHRISTMAS WISHES

Praise for Tammy L. Grace

"*A Season of Hope* is a perfect holiday read! Warm wonderful and gentle tale reflecting small town romance at its best."
    — *Jeanie, review of A Season for Hope: A Christmas Novella*

"This book is a clean, simple romance with a background story very similar to the works of Debbie Macomber. If you like Macomber's books you will like this one. The main character, Hope and her son Jake are on a road trip when their car breaks down, thus starts the story. A holiday tale filled with dogs, holiday fun, and the joy of giving will warm your heart."
    — *Avid Mystery Reader, review of A Season for Hope: A Christmas Novella*

"This book was just as enchanting as the others. Hardships with the love of a special group of friends. I recommend the series as a must read. I loved every exciting moment. A new author for me. She's fabulous."
    —*Maggie!, review of Pieces of Home: A Hometown Harbor Novel (Book 4)*

"Tammy is an amazing author, she reminds me of Debbie Macomber... Delightful, heartwarming...just down to earth."
    — *Plee, review of A Promise of Home: A Hometown Harbor Novel (Book 3)*

"This was an entertaining and relaxing novel. Tammy Grace has a simple yet compelling way of drawing the reader into the lives of her characters. It was a pleasure to read a story that didn't rely on theatrical tricks, unrealistic events or steamy sex scenes to fill up the pages. Her characters and plot were strong enough to hold the reader's interest."

—*MrsQ125, review of Finding Home: A Hometown Harbor Novel (Book 1)*

"This is a beautifully written story of loss, grief, forgiveness and healing. I believe anyone could relate to the situations and feelings represented here. This is a read that will stay with you long after you've completed the book."

—*Cassidy Hop, review of Finally Home: A Hometown Harbor Novel (Book 5)*

Killer Music and Deadly Connection are award-winning novels, earning the 2016 & 2017 Mystery Gold Medal by the Global E-Book Awards

"Killer Music is a clever and well-crafted whodunit. The vivid and colorful characters shine as the author gradually reveals their hidden secrets—an absorbing page-turning read."

— *Jason Deas, bestselling author of Pushed and Birdsongs*

"I could not put this book down! It was so well written & a suspenseful read! This is definitely a 5-star story! I'm hoping there will be a sequel!"

—*Colleen, review of Killer Music*

"This is the best book yet by this author. The plot was well crafted with an unanticipated ending. I like to try to leap ahead and see if I can accurately guess the outcome. I was able to predict some of the plot but not the actual details which made reading the last several chapters quite engrossing."

—*0001PW, review of Deadly Connection*

CHRISTMAS WISHES

SOUL SISTERS AT CEDAR MOUNTAIN LODGE
BOOK 3

TAMMY L. GRACE

LONE MOUNTAIN PRESS

Christmas Wishes
Soul Sisters at Cedar Mountain Lodge, Book 3
Tammy L. Grace

Published in the United States by Lone Mountain Press, Nevada
ISBN 978-1-945591-17-4 (paperback)
FIRST EDITION
Printed in the United States of America

For my author sisters, who make this journey much more fun.

ALSO BY TAMMY L. GRACE

COOPER HARRINGTON DETECTIVE NOVELS

Killer Music

Deadly Connection

Dead Wrong

HOMETOWN HARBOR SERIES

Hometown Harbor: The Beginning (FREE Prequel Novella)

Finding Home

Home Blooms

A Promise of Home

Pieces of Home

Finally Home

Forever Home

CHRISTMAS NOVELLAS

A Season for Hope: Christmas in Silver Falls Book 1

The Magic of the Season: Christmas in Silver Falls Book 2

Christmas in Snow Valley: A Hometown Christmas Novella

GLASS BEACH COTTAGE SERIES

Beach Haven

WRITING AS CASEY WILSON

A Dog's Hope

A Dog's Chance

Tammy would love to connect with readers on social media and her website at https://www.tammylgrace.com. **Remember to subscribe to her mailing list at** https://wp.me/P9umIy-e

and you'll receive the exclusive interview she did with all the canine characters in her Hometown Harbor Series as a thank you gift.

Follow Tammy on Facebook, by liking her author page. You may also follow Tammy on Amazon or at BookBub by clicking on the follow button.

PROLOGUE

Mrs. Ashburn plucked the glasses from the beaded chain around her neck, where they rested against her drab blouse, and perched them on the end of her nose. Her eyes scanned the note in her hand and then flicked over the top of her glasses. "Miss O'Malley," she hollered. "You're to take your things and report to the office."

Her not so subtle announcement elicited snickers and giggles from the class. Jo didn't bother saying goodbye to any of her classmates before trudging down the hallway to her locker and stuffing the library books she had picked up at lunch into her worn backpack. She grabbed the one strap still attached to the top, and let the frayed one drag along the tile floor.

Laughter and merriment spilled from the classrooms into the hallway as classes held their holiday celebrations. Despite the buzz of excitement around Jo, worry and angst filled her thoughts.

The bag was heavy and she took her time getting to the office at Granite Ridge High. Marjorie, the secretary who had known her grandmother smiled at Jo, but it was a pity smile. Jo's heart pounded in her chest. What could she have done to warrant a summons to the office? It couldn't be an overdue meal bill since as humiliating as it was, she was on free lunch now.

Marjorie's eyes darted to the far corner of the office. Mrs. Wacker, her social worker stood there. Her weary eyes gave Jo the same uninspired look she always displayed. "Josephine," she said.

Jo rolled her eyes. *Why can she never remember to call me Jo?* As Jo grumbled, she noticed her tattered cloth bag from Mountain Drugs & Books in Mrs. Wacker's fleshy hand. She had that huggable body shape that made you think of a sweet grandma who loved to bake and cuddle, but she'd never offered Jo so much as an ounce of kindness.

"I had Marjorie send someone to collect your gym clothes." The social worker, bundled in a heavy coat, dipped her head in Marjorie's direction and ushered Jo into the main hallway toward the entrance. "I've got some unexpected news."

Dread crept up Jo's neck. She shoved the door open and a blast of cold air sucked away what little breath she had left.

Mrs. Wacker toddled across the sidewalk, breathing heavily. "I know you haven't been happy at the Monroe's ranch."

That was the understatement of the year. Mr. and Mrs. Monroe were leeches who made it clear they took in foster kids for the money and for what Jo thought of as slave labor at their ranch. Jo had been telling Wacker the Slacker and anyone else who would listen about their fraudulent activities for the last year.

Mrs. Wacker pointed at her dingy gray sedan with government plates. She unlocked it and reached into the backseat. "I picked up your things from the ranch," she said, holding the trash bag up like a trophy.

Jo's head swiveled around the parking lot, looking to see if anyone was watching her and the depressing bag that represented her meager belongings. "Could you please put it in the car before anyone sees?" Jo shook her head with disgust and flung her backpack next to the trash bag, before getting into the passenger seat.

Mrs. Wacker situated her bulk behind the wheel and let out a long sigh. "For reasons I cannot discuss, Mr. and Mrs. Monroe are no longer certified foster parents."

Jo fingered the bandage on her hand and suppressed a smile. The injury from the hay hook had required treatment at urgent care, which had meant a report of the incident to Mrs. Wacker. Jo also made sure her guidance counselor at the high school saw it and knew what had happened. Jo knew full well what could not be discussed. She had lived it for the last year.

"I'm driving you to your new home where you'll meet your new foster mother, Mrs. Kirby."

The momentary elation was fleeting. Jo swallowed a lump in her throat. "What about Nathan and Molly? Where are they going?" Jo's throat burned and her mouth went dry, as if she hasn't tasted water in days. "I can't leave them there. I won't."

Mrs. Wacker's frosted pink lips curved between her pudgy cheeks. "Don't get upset, Josephine." She reached to pat Jo's arm.

"It's Jo," she said, through gritted teeth. "I've told you that for a year and you never remember."

Mrs. Wacker tsked. "I can't possibly remember everyone's nickname now, can I?" She steered the car from the school and added, "You really need to control your temper, my dear. Nathan and Molly's aunt agreed to take them. They're on their way to Boise to get a flight to Kentucky. Placing kids with someone in the family is really the ideal situation." Mrs. Wacker beamed with delight, as if she had been the one to orchestrate such a success.

"Unless, of course, you don't have any family," Jo mumbled. She turned and looked out the window, letting her breath fog it as she took in the festive decorations along Main

Street and the smiling townsfolk milling about the sidewalks, toting holiday shopping bags.

"I didn't even get to say goodbye to them," she whispered. But that was nothing new. They were just the latest in a string of people in her life who had disappeared without a word.

The brakes on Mrs. Wacker's sedan squealed as she parked in front of a huge brick Victorian home. Colorful lights graced the intricate roofline and wrapped around the columns on the porch. The resemblance to one of those fancy gingerbread houses Jo had seen on television wasn't lost on her. The door held a huge fresh wreath and the glow of warm lights filled every window, even the ones in the turret that rose above the highest roof peak.

Her cheeks flushed with embarrassment as she lugged the trash bag and her ratty backpack up the steps. Mrs. Wacker ambled after her, clutching the bag of dirty gym clothes to her chest. When she made it to the porch, she used her gloved finger to poke the doorbell. A soft series of chimes drifted from inside the house.

The door opened and a woman with gentle brown eyes and a warm smile greeted them, along with the mouth-watering aroma of freshly baked sugar cookies, bringing Grandma Maeve immediately to mind. But that's where the similarity ended. The woman was tall, and wore stylish heeled boots, jeans, and a teal green poncho with a shimmery fringe over a matching turtleneck. Jo studied her face, thinking she recognized her, barely listening as Mrs. Wacker droned on making introductions.

Mrs. Kirby extended her hand, revealing a sparkly silver and teal beaded bracelet, and offered to take Jo's backpack. "Let me help you with your things, Jo?"

When Jo heard her voice, she realized why Mrs. Kirby seemed familiar. She was a school counselor at Jo's old school. Jo remembered her as friendly and nice, although she never had much interaction with her. She smiled back at Mrs. Kirby and said, "Yes, and thank you."

Mrs. Wacker stuffed the cloth bag in Jo's arms, promised she'd be in touch after the first of the year, and scurried down the steps. Jo ignored her, focusing instead on the breathtaking entryway and huge staircase, draped with greenery.

Mrs. Kirby led Jo up the staircase. "I don't know if Mrs. Wacker told you, but I've decided to open my home to four children, all girls. You're the oldest, so I wanted you to have this room up here adjacent to the turret, so you'll have some privacy."

She waved her hand around the space outfitted with built in bookshelves filled with leather bound books, a huge desk, and oversized chairs. "This was Mr. Kirby's office, so it's a bit masculine, but I love the dark colors and it gets plenty of light from all the windows." Jo detected sadness in her voice when she mentioned her husband and realized despite her friendly smile, there was a hint of sorrow in Mrs. Kirby's eyes.

Jo looked around the space again. She didn't care what color the furnishings were and imagined herself lounging in the comfortable chair, reading a book by the fire. She followed Mrs. Kirby to the bedroom and gazed at the room decorated in shades of pale and dark green. A thick area rug covered part of the hardwood floor and she took care not to walk on it. The room resembled those she imagined when reading her beloved novels of Jane Austen and Emily Bronte.

She dropped the trash bag on the floor. "My clean clothes have been jumbled with my dirty ones. Do you have a washing machine I could use?"

"Of course, I'll show you the laundry room and how to work the machines. In the meantime, I got you an early

Christmas gift." She removed a package with shimmering ribbons from the dresser and handed it to Jo.

Tears stung Jo's eyes as she read the glittery card attached to the box. *Merry Christmas, Jo. I hope this is the first of many we will spend together. With love, Mrs. Kirby.*

Maybe this was more than a temporary placement. Jo's heart raced at the thought of being able to live in a home like this one with someone who seemed to truly care about her. Someone with a kind heart and room for four foster girls.

She opened the box, taking care to save the gorgeous ribbon, and unearthed a pair of shearling lined boots. She hadn't had new shoes or clothes since before Grandma Maeve had passed away, and let her fingers run over the soft boots.

The hand-me-downs she wore each day to school were becoming more and more threadbare, and her tennis shoes were almost completely worn. "If you don't like them or they don't fit, we can take them back and get something else. I thought we'd go shopping once the other girls arrive and you can all pick out some new jeans and sweaters or whatever else you need." Mrs. Kirby smiled, but looked uneasy, as if she wasn't sure Jo liked the boots.

"They're beautiful. I love them. I, uh, just didn't expect them," Jo said, wiping a finger under her eye.

Mrs. Kirby's smile deepened. "Oh, good, I wasn't sure. Like I said, they're easy to exchange if they don't fit." She showed Jo where things were located and gave her a quick tour of the space. "I'll give you some time to get settled and then just come downstairs. I've got dinner about ready and then you can do your laundry, read, watch television, whatever you'd like. If you're tired, you can make it an early night."

Jo noticed a selection of skin care products and the ointment and bandages on the counter in the bathroom, amazed that Mrs. Kirby had thought of everything she needed. She hurried back to the bedroom and tried on the boots, finding fluffy socks wedged into each toe. She pulled off the ones she wore, with holes in each heel. The boots were warm and so comfortable.

Despite wanting to toss her old shoes and socks, she added them to the trash bag, not convinced this home would last long and not wanting to throw away anything she might need later. Holey socks and too short pants were better than none.

The bed, with a fluffy comforter the color of cream and a beautiful velvety throw in forest green, beckoned her to try it and she rested her head against the pillows, letting her body relax for the first time since she had been placed in care. She shut her eyes, hoping this wasn't just a Christmas placement, knowing full well how some people felt guilty during the holidays and wanted to treat foster kids to something special. She wanted to believe what Mrs. Kirby had written in her card was genuine.

The next day, Jo slept in and then lost herself in Mr. Kirby's bookshelves, running her fingers across the soft, leather-bound volumes. The comfortable space, where the almost musty aroma of the older books mingled with the rich scent of the leather furniture, was Jo's idea of heaven. She lingered there until the sound of the doorbell chimes interrupted her musings and she hustled from the study and down the stairs.

When she arrived, Mrs. Kirby was ushering in three girls, all of them wide-eyed. Jo's heart broke when she saw the youngest one, Hailey, a tiny girl with glasses, no more than second grade, like Molly had been. At least Jo hadn't had to go into foster care until she was older. She couldn't imagine spending her entire childhood like she had spent the last year.

Next, Mrs. Kirby introduced Stevie, who towered over the two younger girls. Freckles dotted her face, framed by fiery red hair, and there was a harshness in her stance and wariness in her eyes that signaled the thirteen-year-old didn't trust easily.

The sweet and petite girl next to her was ten-year-old Alissa. Her big brown eyes were the size of saucers. The two youngest held their trash bags close to them, clinging to what was familiar, uncertainty conveyed in tiny creases in their foreheads.

Mrs. Kirby was gentle with them and took each of the younger girls by the hand, talking in a soft and reassuring voice. After the initial greetings, Jo followed everyone upstairs, carrying Alissa's and Hailey's bags. While the girls explored their rooms and situated their belongings, rather than stand around and gawk at them, Jo sunk into the chair in the study, and picked up the book she had been reading. After everyone had settled into their rooms and gotten acquainted with the layout, Mrs. Kirby suggested they head downstairs to dinner.

Mrs. Kirby led them through the foyer, past the formal dining room and the family room where a huge tree stood next to a window, and into the large kitchen. Last night, Jo had been in a fog, overwhelmed by all the changes, the idea of staying with Mrs. Kirby, and imagining what the three girls might be like, and hadn't taken the time to notice much beyond her bedroom and the study.

Now, past the shock of it all, she surveyed the space in more detail. Everywhere Jo looked, there were beautiful Christmas decorations, twinkling lights, and the whole house smelled of fresh pine. In the corner, a casual wooden table with built in bench seating, decorated with holiday pillows, was set for dinner. Jo had never seen a more beautiful home and hoped again that this wasn't just a temporary placement.

Mrs. Kirby directed the girls to a sink in the mud room where they could wash their hands before taking a seat at the table. Stevie stood in front of the huge granite counter and offered to help Mrs. Kirby with preparations. Jo took charge of the younger girls and got them situated at the table, pouring milk into their glasses, and pointing out some of the beautiful decorations and ornaments tucked in every corner.

Jo marveled at the matching plates and silverware and the fresh flowers in the center of the table. The roast chicken and vegetables were flavorful and delicious. At Mrs. Kirby's urging, she stuffed herself with a second helping of mashed potatoes and gravy. After the meal, Mrs. Kirby said she'd like each of the girls to write a letter to Santa.

Jo offered to help with the dishes, but Mrs. Kirby told her to relax instead and that there would be plenty of time to figure out household chores and responsibilities, but for tonight she only needed to write her letter. Mrs. Kirby bent closer to Jo and whispered, "I know you may not believe in Santa, but help me keep the magic alive for Alissa and Hailey."

Jo took a piece of paper and a pencil and wandered into the family room, next to the tree. As she listened to the soft Christmas music coming from the speakers, she contemplated what to write. She hadn't believed in Santa for several years, but despite her disbelief, her grandma had always made sure she received a special gift from the jolly elf. She felt the tightness in her throat and the sting of tears. This time of year was tough without Grandma Maeve.

Dear Santa, I feel more than silly doing this, since I know you're not real and I'm too old to believe in you, but I can tell writing down my Christmas wish is important to Mrs. Kirby. More than anything, I'd like this feeling I have right now, the one where I am safe and it feels like this could be home and I'm not alone, but have a real family and sisters, to last forever.

In the days that followed, leading up to Christmas, Jo began to feel more at ease. As they shared meals and visited, the girls relaxed more, and the anxious eyes Jo had faced when the other three girls had arrived, had been replaced by smiles and even some giggles from the two youngest.

Mrs. Kirby suggested a trip to town so they could all do a bit of secret Christmas shopping for each other. They strolled through the stores and as they walked, Mrs. Kirby chatted with them about things they liked and pointed out items on the shelves to see what sparked an interest in each of the girls. After they wandered together a bit, Mrs. Kirby gave Jo and Stevie the freedom to duck into the shops along Main Street, giving each of them some money so they could pick out gifts for the others.

When Jo walked into Mountain Drugs and Books, she shut her eyes and thought back to all the times she and Grandma Maeve had spent in the store. If she didn't think too hard, and let the scents from the perfumes and lotions, from the sugared candies lined up along the counter in big glass jars, permeate her senses, she could almost believe it was years ago. Those familiar scents and the underlying essence of new books comforted her. She had missed spending time downtown, going to Rusty's Café for pie, and lingering at the library or plopping into a chair here in the bookstore and reading all afternoon.

She hadn't been able to do any of those things, much less spend time in town, after being taken in by the Monroe family. She relished the bit of freedom afforded her and lingered over the choices, lost in happier memories as she selected gifts for the girls she had just met, hoping this might not be a dream and they might all be together long after Christmas.

Mrs. Kirby loaded the shopping bags in her car, making sure to keep the bags separate, so there was no chance of peeking. As dusk began to settle over Granite Ridge, she drove them home. Jo couldn't help but smile when Alissa and Hailey gasped, their eyes filled with wonder, when they glimpsed the huge house illuminated with what had to be thousands of festive lights.

Alissa and Hailey pointed at different spots in the yard, calling out their favorite colors and gawking at the rows of lights along the roofline. Their eyes reflected not only the sparkle of the lights, but the true wonder of the season. Jo helped carry the shopping bags and stood at the end of the driveway, captivated by the twinkling display and the warmth that radiated from the glow of soft lights, matched only by the heart of Mrs. Kirby, who smiled as she watched the girls and brushed a finger under her eyes.

Christmas morning, Jo, wearing the new red flannel night-gown she had found under her pillow last night, tiptoed past the closed door of the bedroom shared by Alissa and Hailey, and made her way downstairs. Mrs. Kirby and Stevie were in the kitchen, both donning Christmas aprons over their red flannel nightgowns as they worked at the large granite counter.

"Merry Christmas, Jo," said Mrs. Kirby. "We're just getting breakfast together, so we can have a bite to eat after we open presents."

Listening to Stevie over dinner the last couple of nights, Jo had learned she enjoyed cooking. From the smile on her face as she helped Mrs. Kirby put the finishing touches on a braided pastry, it was evident she was happiest when she was creating something in the kitchen.

The decadent pastry, covered in slivered almonds and powdered sugar, looked delicious, as did the cheesy egg casserole Mrs. Kirby was making. She explained that Mr. Kirby had a tradition of having blueberry waffles on

Christmas morning and hoped the girls would enjoy them. Stevie beamed when she was put in charge of making them.

Soon, they heard Hailey and Alissa scurrying down the stairs. Jo peeked around the corner and spied Hailey, carrying her little stuffed dog, Charlie, and holding hands with Alissa as they both stared at the tree. Both of them fidgeted with excitement to open presents, and couldn't resist touching a few of shiny packages. Jo hated to admit it, but even she was excited to open presents. Last Christmas, the first without Grandma Maeve, had been miserable, but these last few days with Mrs. Kirby gave her a glimmer of hope.

Jo couldn't help but smile and felt Mrs. Kirby's hand on her shoulder as she joined in watching them. Instead of worrying about breakfast, Mrs. Kirby popped the casserole and the pastry into the oven to bake and suggested they open gifts and then enjoy their meal. While Jo took charge of keeping an eye on the two youngest, Stevie made hot chocolate for everyone. Mrs. Kirby added her own mug of hot tea to the tray she carried into the family room, where the girls sat cross-legged in front of the tree, anxiously waiting, while they eyed the tags on the mountain of gifts under the tree.

Mrs. Kirby passed out the gifts and asked all the girls to watch as each one opened their boxes. Shrieks of delight came from Alissa and Hailey as they opened their puzzles, books, pens, and pencils. Like the other girls, Jo had taken the money Mrs. Kirby had given her and tried to find meaningful gifts, keeping in mind Hailey's affection for dogs, Stevie's ambitions in the kitchen, and Alissa's love of books. Choosing Mrs. Kirby's gift was harder, but Jo settled on a rhinestone encrusted picture frame and included a note that it was meant to hold a photo of all of them celebrating their first Christmas together.

Jo treasured the hair ribbon from Hailey, the journal from Alissa, and the fancy gourmet fudge from Stevie, along with the sturdy new backpack from Mrs. Kirby. More than the gifts, she cherished the tender smiles from each of them. These three girls had found a way into her heart, and along with the kind woman who had opened her home to all of them, they already felt like family.

When Mrs. Kirby opened Jo's gift, tears dotted her cheeks. She gathered the girls closer to her, scrunching them together by stretching her arms around them, and used her phone to capture the moment. She gazed at the photo and said, "This is so very special and is the true meaning of Christmas. I'm so thankful you're all here to spend it with me." She clutched the frame to her chest. "You don't know how much this means to me. We'll have to take our picture every year, just like this one."

From the little things Mrs. Kirby mentioned and the way she spoke about their future, Jo sensed that Mrs. Kirby needed the four girls as much as they needed her.

After they finished the yummy breakfast, Jo and Stevie did the dishes and cleaned up the kitchen, while Mrs. Kirby got the younger girls organized and ready to meet Mrs. Kirby's mother, Claire, who was due to arrive later in the morning.

After, Jo went upstairs to her room and dressed in a new sweater, a deep copper color that brought out the highlights in her brown hair, then she took her new journal to the over-sized chair near the bookcase in Mr. Kirby's office. She had already placed her beloved copy of *To Kill A Mockingbird* that Grandma Maeve had given her on one of the shelves, and now was anxious to read the leather volume resting next to it.

Mrs. Kirby shared that her husband had been a professor in the philosophy department and had amassed a huge collection of books, and that Jo was welcome to read any of them. Jo had chosen *Middlemarch*, fascinated by the idea of a woman writing under a man's name, and was eyeing the Shakespeare collection for her next read. She slouched across the chair, letting her legs dangle over the arm. Quickly, she admired her new boots, then checked the time. Mrs. Kirby's mother, who hoped the girls would call her Nan, was due to arrive in a few minutes. Jo wrote the date at the top of the first page of her journal before jotting an entry.

I think my letter to Santa worked. This last year has eaten away at me. I wasn't convinced I could trust Mrs. Kirby, but she's given me new hope. Her genuine kindness and love shine through in all that she does for us. She's patient and warm, but isn't going to put up with any shenanigans, as Grandma Maeve would say. She wants us to be a family, soul sisters, she says. She explained although we aren't related by blood, the term means we're kindred spirits and we'll always be linked by a bond that transcends time and distance. I like the idea that no matter what happens, we'll always have each other. I've felt lonely for so long, except for Grandma Maeve, and losing her made me realize just how harsh the world can be. I didn't think anyone cared and that no one ever would again. But now I have sisters. Sisters of my heart. I have a family! Please, please, please, make it be real.

CHAPTER 1

Jo's cell phone chimed and she saw her mom's name on the screen. It had taken Jo a long time to refer to Maddie, the woman who adopted her when she was sixteen, as Mom, and she still called her Maddie at times. She had never called anyone else Mom, or at least never remembered doing so. Jo's memories of her birth mother were limited to photos, since she had died before Jo had a chance to know her. From all accounts, she wasn't deserving of the title. She had overdosed and it was never determined if it was accidental or an act of suicide. Regardless of the intent, her mother's death had set Jo on a path that ultimately led to her being in foster care.

Her dad, Joseph, was in the military and had been called back with the sad news. He wasn't in a position to care for a small child on his own, schlepping from base to base. Grandma Maeve, her dad's mother, had come to the rescue, taking Jo in and raising her as her own. Life with her grandmother had been happy and carefree, although she missed seeing her dad. He came home to Granite Ridge a few times each year, but never for long.

Grandma Maeve was the librarian in Granite Ridge and Jo

15

had spent many hours helping shelve books and losing herself within the pages of others. Grandma wasn't rich by any means, but was comfortable and what she couldn't provide in the way of material objects, she more than made up for with the time she dedicated to Jo.

Being an only child, Jo spent most of her free time with adults, and having Grandma for a guardian meant she spent it with more mature adults. She credited that and all the hours she spent reading, with her robust vocabulary and quick mind, not to mention her even quicker tongue. Often, Grandma had to remind her she was not an adult and while she was free to have opinions, not everyone was as open or interested in them as Grandma. That may have explained Jo's lack of close friends during her school years. She had no interest in their juvenile pursuits and elected to spend time with Grandma Maeve and her friends or with her imaginary friends in books.

Then, soon after Jo's eighth birthday, the day military families dread, arrived. Grandma Maeve received the news that her only son, Joseph Daniel O'Malley, had been killed in action. The loss of her son was hard on her, but she and Jo persevered, got through the funeral, and moved on with their lives.

Six years later, when Grandma Maeve suddenly died, that's when Jo's world began to unravel. There were no other relatives to turn to and Jo was relegated to the foster system. She had endured a year of living with strangers, the last of whom were eventually deemed unfit, thanks to Jo's own intervention. Nobody seemed to care or listen to her when she wrote letters and aired her concerns. She still remembered portly old Mrs. Wacker, her social worker, who was better fit for a job behind a counter in a shop or as a telemarketer, where her actions or more likely lack of such, wouldn't impact any living thing.

Things changed when Jo was taken to Mrs. Kirby's house

right before Christmas that first year. Unsure if it would last, but hoping the kind woman's home would be more than just a temporary holiday placement, Jo met the three younger girls – Stevie, Alissa, and Hailey. The women she now called her sisters. That first Christmas, Maddie explained they would be soul sisters and the bond they felt would always be theirs.

Seeing that one word on her phone, "Mom", brought all those old memories rushing back to Jo. The call wasn't unexpected. With Alissa's wedding scheduled for Christmas Eve, Jo's phone had been pinging with texts from her sisters and mom for the last several weeks, checking on details.

Jo had picked up her long silvery gray bridesmaid dress on her lunch hour and it was hanging on the back of her office door, along with the matching sparkly shoes and soft faux fur wrap she had purchased. Maddie had been concerned she might forget the dress, so Jo smiled when she answered.

"I have the dress and my shoes. I'm looking at them right now. No need to worry." Jo glanced at the framed photo on her desk and reached to touch the smooth metal. Although the quality of the photo wasn't great, Jo treasured it. It had been with her for fifteen years and she remembered that feeling when Maddie hugged them all close and snapped the photo on her phone. The smiling faces of her sisters with their mom in the midst, even all these years later, brought a smile to her face.

"Oh, sweetie, I wish this was a call just to nag you about that. Um, I've got some bad news." Maddie's normally enthusiastic voice cracked.

"What's wrong? What's happened?" Jo's forehead creased with worry and she poised her pen over her notepad, tapping it on the paper.

"Jed called off the wedding. Alissa is devastated and heartbroken. She's not up to talking to everyone about it just yet. She also feels guilty, since there's no way to get our money back on anything."

Jo had sent a sizeable check to help with the costs when Jed's family, owners of a very lucrative spirits company in Seattle, had refused to be involved and had in essence boycotted the entire event. Maddie and the other three sisters insisted they would pitch in and help to make sure Alissa had the wedding of her dreams. Maddie and Nan did the bulk of the heavy lifting, but Jo's career afforded her the luxury of being able to cover a substantial amount of the costs and she had been happy to help.

The pen Jo was holding beat faster, pounding the notepad with sharp whacks. Jo had a whisper of a bad feeling about this from the beginning, when she learned that despite their wealth, Jed's parents would not contribute or help in any way. She knew Alissa had been deemed an ill fit for their golden only child. They must have upped the pressure they had been applying to Jed and he cracked.

"Poor Alissa. I can't believe he would wait until now to end it. He must know nothing is refundable at this late date. Although, when you're used to working with billions, what's a few thousand? Especially when it's not your money. We could probably sue him and recoup some of it."

Jo listened to Maddie's deep sigh. "Whoa, let's not go down that road. I've assured Alissa the money doesn't matter, so don't bring it up. She feels bad enough already. Could you call Stevie and let her know? Maybe use your influence to keep her calm. Goodness knows what she'll think is an appropriate reaction. She's liable to show up at Jed's house with a baseball bat or something. This is such a sad and disappointing turn of events."

"Yeah, I'll call Stevie. Don't worry."

"Listen, you've already got time off and your ticket booked. It's been forever since you've spent more than a few days with all of us. Alissa is here. I think we should go ahead up to Cedar Mountain Lodge and stay for the holidays, like we planned. Take time, let Alissa lick her wounds, surrounded by her family. We could enjoy all the fun activities going on up at the lodge. Do whatever we want, have some downtime, enjoy the gorgeous setting, and the fun New Year's Eve party they always host. It's all paid for and I think we might as well enjoy it."

Jo heard the longing and uptick in Maddie's voice, full of hope. She was worried about Alissa and wanted all her chicks back in the nest, together for her sake and Alissa's. Maddie was right, Jo had been laser focused on her career at Hale and Gray, moving up in the ranks, living carefully, and socking away most of her salary in her investment accounts. This was the first actual vacation she had scheduled. She took a few days off here and there, when Stevie showed up to visit, out of the blue, with her motorhome, or when Alissa came over the summer, but never two weeks off away from the city.

Sometimes, Jo felt like she and Maddie co-parented the other three girls. Jo was the oldest, thirty this year, and like Grandma Maeve used to say, she had been born an old soul. Most people that worked with her or met her, assumed she was a least ten years older. It wasn't due to her appearance, but her serious nature and wisdom beyond her years.

Jo had spent the least amount of time with Maddie and although ashamed of it, was sometimes jealous of the other girls, who had the benefit of being with her for so much longer. Hailey still lived in Granite Ridge, so she got to see Maddie all the time. Alissa was in Seattle and could make the short trip for a weekend visit. Stevie traveled for seasonal cooking work at various resorts, but came home to Granite Ridge often. Jo was the only one who lived so far away from home. She had been an excellent student and with Maddie's help and nurturing she excelled further and secured a scholarship to college, went on to obtain her law degree, and enjoyed success at the firm she had been with since law school.

That same drive that pushed Jo to be self-reliant at fifteen, was still with her and her quest for a secure future, one where she wouldn't have to rely on anyone, consumed her and left little time for a social life. Any time she had away from her office, was spent at Love Links, the organization where Jo volunteered to help foster children and where she felt the most gratified, using her legal skills to help those who needed them most.

Losing Grandma Maeve and being at the mercy of the system had left Jo with not just a desire, but more of a crusade to embark on a career that would allow her to amass wealth and secure her future. She had gained a family, sisters, a mom, even a grandma in Maddie's mother, Nan, but she would never again be reliant on anyone but herself.

She had been looking forward to this trip, the chance to visit with everyone, be surrounded by the love of her sisters and Mom. "I think that sounds great. I've been looking forward to relaxing for two weeks." Jo glanced at the dress. "I guess there's no point in bringing the dress and all the paraphernalia that goes with it?"

"Sadly, the dress won't be needed. I know that won't break your heart, since you're not one that likes to dress up in fancy clothes. You can kick back and relax, enjoy a well-deserved vacation. I can't wait to see you and have all my girls together again."

Jo promised to make the call to Stevie, confirmed she'd meet up with everyone at the lodge the day after tomorrow, and disconnected.

She took a deep breath and scrolled to Stevie's name. Looking at the time, she realized she only had a few minutes before a meeting. She poked the green button and listened to Stevie's voicemail greeting. Instead of a message, Jo tapped out a text.

Mom just called and said Jed cancelled the wedding. Before you decide to do anything rash, think of Alissa and Mom. Alissa is struggling and very upset. We don't need to do anything that will make her feel worse. Mom thinks we should all go ahead as planned and stay at the lodge over the holidays. I agree and am looking forward to seeing you all the day after tomorrow. We can cheer Alissa up and have a nice long visit. Bonus: I don't have to wear the dress! Heading to a meeting, talk soon. Love you, Jo.

Jo plucked the file from her desk, took her notepad, and left her cell phone. As she walked down the hall to the conference room, she hoped Stevie would heed her words and not do or say anything to exacerbate the situation. Who was she kidding? Stevie wasn't known for her subtlety.

CHAPTER 2

The next morning, Jo woke to find a late-night text from Stevie. Along with some colorful language about Jed and what Stevie would like to do to him. The shocking image made Jo laugh, but also twitch at the ache in the middle of her chest. In addition to feeling sorry for Alissa, it was a disappointment knowing Stevie's time had been wasted and her beautiful creation wouldn't be enjoyed by everyone. Although Stevie had what Jo called a hard, outer shell, she was a bit of a marshmallow on the inside. She poured her heart into everything she cooked and if you were lucky enough to be a guest at her table or receive one of her desserts, you could taste the love in every bite.

Of all the girls, Stevie was the only one with a living parent. Not that she would refer to her birth mother as a true mother. Her mother had done a number on her and seemed to enjoy tying Stevie in knots and playing with her emotions. She abandoned Stevie when she was just thirteen and then had the audacity to try and take her back from Maddie. Even while in high school, Jo helped research cases and encouraged Stevie to tell the court she wanted to stay with Mrs. Kirby. Stevie was torn. Her mother succeeded in gaining custody, but only briefly, before abandoning her again. She still popped into Stevie's life, like a virus, every year or so, unexpectedly, always wreaking havoc and reminding Stevie of what she didn't want to be.

Jo texted back a smiley face and reminded her it was better that Jed broke it off now instead of waiting until after they were married. She also told her she was expecting to gorge herself on the irresistible cookies she always made for the holidays. Baking and cooking soothed Stevie and Jo knew the best salve for her wounds would be found in the kitchen.

Jo was amazed at what Stevie could prepare in her tiny kitchen. She lived in an old Toyota motorhome that she adored and had remodeled. It was beyond cute, done up with new appliances, flooring, and gleaming white counters. It had a farmhouse vibe and Stevie had added colorful touches in her bedding and throw pillows that decorated the built-in dinette seating. It was small, but gave Stevie the freedom she loved. She even had an electric bike that she hauled around with her, equipped with a large basket for hauling groceries and Ed, her precious–and ancient–terrier mix dog. Jo felt another pang. *Used* to haul Ed around. He had died not long ago and Stevie had been brokenhearted.

Stevie enjoyed the nomadic life and had even worked on a cruise ship. Unlike Jo, she loved a spontaneous adventure and the ability to go wherever she liked, without anything to tie her down. Jo knew she spent time at Maddie's, staying for days or weeks at time, using her kitchen, treating her to gourmet meals and cleaning her house, while Maddie worked.

Hailey, a librarian by day and a secret author by night, published her books under a pen name using tight contracts Jo had devised, so that her name or likeness was never associated with the books. Nobody, outside of her family and any close friends she chose to tell, knew about her success. When Hailey published a new book, Maddie always made an event out of it and had a celebration for her at the house. Stevie would concoct some delicious finger foods or desserts and they would enjoy the celebration, admiring Hailey's beautiful children's stories.

Along with birthday celebrations and other family events, Alissa made it home for these book parties, but usually it was impossible for Jo to make the trip and she only visited at Christmas, joining in the fun via video chat when she could. Jo envied the time they were all able to spend together and sometimes when she was especially lonely, staring at the walls in her quiet apartment, she secretly longed to live in Granite Ridge, under the protection of Maddie's roof. The problem was, there were no suitable jobs and there was no way she could make the salary she was making in Chicago.

The non-wedding news had thrown a wrench into Jo's Christmas gift for Alissa. Each year, like that very first year Maddie had taken them shopping to pick out gifts for each other, the sisters exchanged Christmas presents. It wasn't about big and flashy or expensive, more about the thought and meaning behind the gift. Jo had already wrapped the custom wooden desk nameplate she had ordered for Alissa. She couldn't give her something that said "Mrs. Marsh" now that she wouldn't be married.

Today the firm was closing at noon for their annual holiday party they were hosting, starting at three o'clock. That gave Jo a few hours to pick up the colorful floral clogs she had ordered for Stevie and the personalized leather journal for Hailey. She thought they were perfect gifts for the chef who spent too many hours on her feet and the author who never seemed to run out of ideas she needed to jot down.

Unlike Jo, Maddie was always fashionable with stylish clothes and accessories to match. This year, Jo had found a gorgeous silver bracelet, consisting of five thin bangles, one a bit wider that Jo had engraved with a quote – *Whether side by side or miles apart, we'll always be linked by our hearts.* The name of each sister was inscribed on the other skinnier bangles and a tiny silver heart engraved with "soul sisters" linked the shiny bracelets together. She knew Maddie would love it and it would go with everything.

As soon as the office closed, she activated the out of office message on her desk phone and email, replaced her work shoes with tennis shoes, and set out to run her errands. Thankful all she had left to do was attend the holiday party at the office and not the extravagant gala the firm put on for all the employees at a posh hotel on the Gold Coast tomorrow night. This year, she had the perfect excuse of being out of town.

As she picked up the gifts, she wracked her brain to think of something new for Alissa. She was a kindergarten teacher, loved kids and dogs, and lived in a suburb outside of Seattle, close to where she lived as a child before her parents died. After browsing several stores, she settled on some adult coloring books, several dog-themed and a few with landscapes and landmarks associated with the Pacific Northwest. She added sets of pens and pencils, along with a selection of teas and a new mug. She knew, from personal experience, that coloring was quite soothing during times of stress and figured Alissa could use the distraction. The gift wasn't near as thoughtful as the nameplate, but there was little time to come up with anything better.

She stopped at one of her favorite cafes on the way back to her apartment for lunch. After she finished her soup and chunk of fresh bread, she hurried home to wrap the presents and change for the party.

She had settled on a festive looking emerald colored blouse Maddie had helped her pick out during a shopping video chat. She had told Jo the color brought out her eyes and reminded her it matched a necklace Maddie had given her for her birthday a few years ago. Jo always wore a business suit to work, with a matching jacket and pants and a conservative shirt or blouse, so the chic blouse was a step outside her comfort zone. She paired the beautiful taffeta blouse with her favorite black pants, added the necklace and sparkly earrings, a pair of open toe black heels, and the soft furry wrap she wouldn't be wearing for the wedding. Might as well get some use out of it.

She normally walked to work, but elected to take a car since it was getting colder and she didn't want the hassle of changing shoes. Jo was dreading the party. In her mind, she committed to staying two hours. Making small talk with clients and coworkers drained her energy. As an introvert, large social gatherings were not her strong suit. She'd rather be at home, curled up with a book or watching a movie.

It wasn't that she didn't like her coworkers. Her assistant, Louise, was terrific and they sometimes grabbed lunch together. She caught the occasional movie with her or Margot, another lawyer who was in the office next to Jo. She'd been to Brandon's house, who occupied the office across the hallway, for dinner several times and enjoyed spending time with his wife, Lauren, who was in finance.

Jo was happiest though, spending time with her neighbor, Doris, who was a widow in her early seventies. She reminded Jo of Grandma Maeve and they often traded books or chatted over tea and cake. Jo ran errands for Doris, especially during the winter when the weather made it difficult for Doris to get outside. They also played Scrabble and Jo had introduced Doris to several of the streaming services, allowing her to watch many of her favorite British mysteries and dramas.

The two neighbors often spent part of the holidays together, but this year, Doris's son insisted she come to Texas and spend a few weeks with them. Doris wasn't looking forward to the trip, but Jo was thankful she had someplace to go where she'd be with family. Jo made a point of checking on her at least once a day and knocked on her door on her way downstairs to catch her ride back to the office.

The door opened to twinkling blue eyes and soft white hair. Doris greeted Jo with a sweet smile. "Oh, you look stunning. You're all set for the party?" The elderly woman stood maybe five feet high and in heels Jo towered over her.

"On my way, just wanted to check in on you. I'm leaving super early in the morning, so won't get a chance to say goodbye. I wanted to wish you a Merry Christmas."

Doris motioned her inside and darted into the kitchen. She returned with a plastic container decorated with red snowflakes. "I made you some snacks to take on the plane tomorrow. The way they run people through like cattle, you don't even get a chance for a decent meal."

Doris promised to see her in January and hugged her goodbye. Jo tightened her squeeze around the petite woman. "Thank you for the thoughtful care package. I'm sure it will come in handy tomorrow."

After depositing the treats on the counter in her apartment, she hurried downstairs and hopped into the waiting car.

The lobby of her office building was already filled with people, milling about, helping themselves to the appetizer stations, and lining up at the open bar.

Jo made her way to her office to stash her wrap and purse. While she had been away, the partners had their elves deliver Christmas goodies, gift baskets, chocolates, and bottles of wine, along with Christmas bonus checks to each of the employees. Her brows rose when she glanced at the electronic deposit receipt inside the holiday envelope. At least they acknowledged her hard work over the past year.

Jo did her best to mingle, greeting clients and dispensing holiday wishes. She spent most of her time perched at one of the small cocktail tables the caterers had brought in, between Margot and Louise, sampling delicious appetizers and bite-sized desserts.

Jo checked her watch and when it reached the two-hour

mark, she navigated back to her office, collected her gifts, including enough bottles of wine to get her through several months, and slipped out using the rear hallway door. The two tote bags she carried were heavy and another reason she had taken the car service. The partners were always generous with the gifts and walking home with them would be impossible.

She lugged everything up to her apartment and after putting things away, changed into warm pajamas, and added the green blouse to her suitcase. Maddie had suggested she bring it in case they elected to have a nice dinner at the lodge. She loved the feel of the furry wrap and placed it beside the blouse.

Without the addition of the long bridesmaid's dress and all the accessories, she had plenty of room in her bag for casual clothes. She tuned the television to a Christmas movie, paired a piece of pumpkin bread from Doris with a cup of hot tea and settled in on the couch, intent on getting to bed early.

CHAPTER 3

I n the dark hours of the morning, sipping her second
cup of coffee, Jo steeled herself for the throng of people
she knew would be at the airport and the harried day of
travel ahead of her. She finished adding a couple more
sweaters and a warm hoodie to her bright red hard sided bag
and zipped it shut, wheeling it next to her worn leather
satchel that rested by the front door. Maddie had given her
the soft bag when she graduated law school and it had been
with her ever since.

Jo's heart ached for Alissa, who didn't deserve the misery
Jed had bestowed upon her with his announcement. She was
such a kind and good-natured woman and Jo knew she
would be heartsick. Maddie was a strong person, having
survived the loss of her husband and daughter, and the
raising of four adopted girls, and yet as she told Jo about the
situation, even her voice had quaked with emotion.

A part of Jo worried that spending time at the lodge
would be too hard for Alissa, but she trusted Maddie's
instincts. She had always done what she thought best for her
girls and she was sure the comfort of her family and all the
festive fun and decorations at the lodge would cheer Alissa.

Jo's phone beeped and a quick glance told her the car service the firm provided was waiting downstairs. Her regular driver, Eddie, made quick work of the trip to the airport, wishing her a Merry Christmas as he carried her bags to the curb.

Despite the early hour, the airport was a frenzy of activity. The line for premier flyers was short and Jo checked her bag at the counter, and since she flew quite often for work and was a TSA precheck member, sailed through the security line. She was in the airline's lounge sipping a cup of Earl Grey with honey within thirty minutes.

She checked her phone before boarding and found a text from Maddie, who was up in the early hours of the morning as well. She wished Jo a safe flight, told her she loved her, and couldn't wait to see her at the lodge. Maddie wasn't sure when everyone would arrive, but suggested dinner once they were all situated.

Jo settled into her first-class seat, courtesy of her mileage points, to Boise, inserted her earbuds and selected the playlist that always reminded her of Maddie. The soulful and somewhat melancholy music of Sarah McLachlan drifted from her phone. Jo hadn't been home since last Christmas and like usual, she had stayed for just a few days before getting back to her work in Chicago. As she listened to the sentimental song, she reflected on those past trips. She always looked forward to going home, but dreaded leaving, which was why she only made the trip at Christmas.

It was too hard to experience so much warmth and joy and then leave it all behind for an empty apartment in the city. She loved being surrounded by her sisters and Maddie, having fun and enjoying the comforts of home, but when it came time to leave, she couldn't handle the overwhelming sadness, knowing she'd be returning to what most people would consider a successful career and life, but in reality, was lonely. Those weeks after Christmas were the hardest for Jo.

The gloomy January weather only intensified her feelings of loss.

The idea of being with her family for two whole weeks was heavenly. Being a teacher, Alissa was off work and always able to stay throughout the holidays. In addition to being an author, Hailey was the children's librarian at the same library Grandma Maeve had run for years. Jo loved visiting the library, walking in and inhaling the scent of all those books. It always brought back happy memories. Hailey usually took time off work and Stevie could do whatever she wanted and always spent her holidays at Maddie's. Jo was the only one who cut her holiday visits short. She vowed to relegate the despair she always associated with having to leave Granite Ridge and Maddie's house to the back of her mind and enjoy every minute this year, trying to live in the moment instead of worrying about the future.

She definitely needed something more upbeat to listen to and flicked the screen of her phone to a new playlist filled with her favorite country songs. The other lawyers in her office didn't understand her taste in music. You could take the small-town girl out of Granite Ridge, but you couldn't take her love for country music out of her. She settled into her seat and let Keith Urban's voice begin to lull her to sleep.

The song reminded her of how much she had been looking forward to the casual rehearsal dinner Alissa told her Jed had planned. Both of them were country music fans and met at a concert. They had decided on an informal beer and barbecue themed rehearsal dinner instead of the over-the-top fancy affair Jo expected from the billionaire family. Of course, that was before Jo knew the extent of his parents' objections. As she drifted off to sleep, she wondered what had happened to make Jed call things off. He had stood strong against his parents for the last year, knowing they didn't approve of Alissa.

She woke up in time to munch on a few of Doris's cookies

and see the majestic snow-covered mountains as the plane descended into Boise. Compared to Chicago, the airport was a breeze. She collected her bag and picked up her rental SUV. The roads were clear, making the two-hour drive uneventful. She couldn't resist a quick detour to drive by Maddie's house.

It didn't disappoint. It reminded her of the first time she saw it, fifteen years ago, lit up with the colorful Christmas lights, still looking like a fancy gingerbread house. Maddie loved decorating for the holidays and with the planned nuptials, Jo was certain she had outdone her usual lavish decking of the halls. She gazed at the windows of her old bedroom and felt a lump in her throat as all the happy memories of her years spent perched under that roof flashed before her.

She steered the SUV back to the main road and drove through town, stopping at the market. She gathered the wine and snacks she knew would be needed to get the women through what were sure to be long discussions about Jed and his family, then headed up the increasingly snow packed road to Cedar Mountain Lodge. As she circled the main driveway, she marveled at the tallest tree, decorated with thousands of lights and garland, in the beautifully landscaped area separating the lodge from Jackson's, the popular pub and live music venue that was a hot spot for visitors and locals.

She parked under the oversized portico, letting the bellman take her bags and the valet handle parking, while she checked in at the reception desk. The lodge was as welcoming as she remembered, decked out in its holiday best with lights wrapping the columns of the entryway and sparkling in the bushes along the path. Wreaths with shimmering red ribbons adorned the huge entry doors and the spicy aroma of warm cider greeted her. Staff members wearing Santa hats and reindeer antlers roamed the space, offering guests fresh cookies, cider, and hot chocolate.

A tall tree, stretched to the apex of the open beamed ceiling, twinkled next to the cozy flames in the huge stone fireplace that took centerstage in the lobby. Fresh greenery adorned every nook and cranny, and the fragrant and clean smell of the pine and spruce trees covering the hills surrounding the lodge, filled the air. While she waited for the clerk, Jo admired the lobby with its walls of glass that offered the stunning views coveted by all who visited. Holiday tunes drifted from the grand piano, providing a touch of Christmas spirit. It would have been the perfect venue for Alissa's ceremony.

Jo eyed the comfy leather chairs and couches sitting atop the thick deep-red area rug that graced the space, and planned to spend a few hours in one very soon.

After getting two room keys, in case Stevie wanted a long shower or a few creature comforts, Jo couldn't resist a warm cookie and a cup of cider from the tray at the reception desk. She climbed the grand staircase, stopping on the landing before heading up to the third floor, to admire the decorations below. Cedar Mountain Lodge was gorgeous no matter the time of the year, but as reflected in the tasteful use of pinecones, lights, fresh greens, and splashes of red, Christmas was a special time.

When she got to her mini suite, her bags were already there waiting. A warm fire glowed in the glass fireplace that could be viewed from the sitting and bedroom areas, and a plush dog bed rested near it. She had arranged for a pet-friendly suite long before Stevie had lost Ed, and had forgotten about it. The tree in the corner of her room twinkled with lights amid sparkling red and white ornaments. Jo let out a sigh of relief and tossed her leather bag on the sofa, then stashed the snacks and wine in the refrigerator. Her stomach rumbled; she needed some real food, instead of all the sweets she'd been packing in all day. She noted the dog bowls and bags of treats for canine guests as she fixed a plate of sliced cheese and apples for a snack that would hold her over until dinner.

Seconds after she texted Maddie with her room number, her phone pinged with a reply. Maddie had to make a late trip to the airport to pick up Nan, whose flight had been delayed. She wouldn't be joining the girls for dinner, but their reservation was set up downstairs in the Cedar Mountain Restaurant. She promised to meet up with everyone in the morning at breakfast.

That gave Jo a few hours, and she elected to use them for a nap. Traveling was exhausting, and she had been up way too early this morning. After setting the alarm on her phone, she tuned the television in the bedroom to the lodge's channel, letting the scenery and descriptions of the activities available to guests soothe her as she drifted to sleep.

Jo was in a deep sleep when the beeping from her phone woke her. Her thick hair needed a bit of help and once she had used the curling iron on it, she changed out of her rumpled clothes, slipping into jeans, a sweater, and warm boots. She hurried downstairs, tempted by the offer of another cookie, but instead made her way to the restaurant. She spotted Stevie's auburn hair piled into a messy bun atop her head at a curved booth in the back of the restaurant. When she rounded the corner, she caught Hailey's eye.

Jo slid into the open spot next to Hailey. Her sister's child-like face and blue eyes reminding Jo of one of the little fairy characters in the children's books Hailey authored. Jo squeezed her hand in a greeting and slipped an arm around her petite shoulders to hug her.

Alissa was sandwiched between Hailey and Stevie and her forced smile couldn't hide her puffy eyes and splotchy cheeks. When Maddie had made the call to Jo, they had agreed to limit any discussion about Jed and not bash on him. There was little point in harping on it and Jo thought it best to chime in only if Alissa brought up the subject.

Hailey wouldn't have a problem, but Stevie would be the wild card in the mix. She had a hard time containing her thoughts. Whatever was on Stevie's mind tumbled out of her mouth. Jo could relate, but she had learned restraint and wielded power with her written words and legal acumen nowadays.

Alissa was quiet throughout dinner, obliging a smile here and there when the sisters said something funny, but her mind was clearly elsewhere. Hailey regaled them with the latest about her new book, her eyes shimmering with excitement when she mentioned the main character, Charlie, and his dog, Zeke. Nobody would ever guess the timid librarian was a hugely successful author of popular children's books cherished around the nation.

Stevie was quieter than normal, heeding the warning Maddie and Jo had given her about keeping her thoughts to herself. Jo enjoyed the delicious meal, but noticed Alissa picked at her food, moving it around on her plate, but barely eating.

After dinner, Stevie and Hailey decided to finish off the evening at the bar. Jo gave Stevie a room key. "Feel free to use it whenever you need to." She hugged both Stevie and Hailey goodbye.

Despite still being tired, Jo walked Alissa back to her room. Poor Alissa, usually so full of life and cheer, seemed to wilt as she opened the heavy door.

Jo poured her sister a glass of wine and they snuggled into the couch. Alissa tucked her dark hair, cut in a cute bob cut that made her seem even younger, behind her ears. Tears pooled in her dark brown eyes. "I'm sure Mom told you, but I want to apologize for all of this. You were so kind to help pay for the wedding and I'm just so sorry it has been wasted. I'm so embarrassed."

Jo slipped a protective arm around her sister. "Don't worry about it. It's not your fault. What's important is you and the fact that we're all here together. We're here for you and we'll never let you down. You know that, right?"

Tears streaked Alissa's cheeks as she nodded, then rested her head against Jo's shoulder. "I can't believe this is happening. It feels like a bad dream. And, I'm ruining Christmas for everyone."

Jo squeezed her closer. "It's not going to be ruined. Everyone is here for you, whatever you need. If you want company, you'll have it. If you want to talk about Jed, we can do that. If you want to forget it all and have fun, that works. You can do whatever feels right, whatever you're up to."

Alissa nodded and moved her head from Jo's shoulder. "I just want to forget him, but I love him."

Jo had a hard time understanding how Alissa could say she still loved him. If someone left her days before her wedding, she'd kick him to the curb or turn Stevie loose on him. But disparaging Jed wouldn't help Alissa feel any better. She let her sister talk, then tuned the television to a seasonal movie, with a guaranteed happy ending. The kind she knew Alissa loved.

Jo's eyes kept fluttering to stay open. "I've got to get back to my room. I was up way too early today." She hugged Alissa and promised to see her tomorrow. At the door, she turned. "Call me, anytime, if you need anything or just to talk."

Back in her room, she practically fell into bed. She felt privileged to be here for Alissa, but holding back her own sadness over her sister's broken heart was exhausting, and her anger toward Jed didn't help either. Alissa was so hurt, and if there was one thing Jo could understand and still, after all these years, feel down to her bones, it was the devastation of loss.

CHAPTER 4

J o was up early and donned her warm walking clothes. With plenty of time before breakfast with her family, she had been looking forward to taking in the beauty of the mountains and trees in the quiet of the morning, and wasn't about to miss her first chance. There were several trails surrounding the property, but since it was still rather dark, she stuck close to the main lodge and the buildings surrounding it, keeping to the lighted pathways.

A peaceful silence greeted her, as did the crisp mountain air. Reflected Christmas lights glowed on the fresh snow that had fallen last night. The grounds workers were in the process of clearing it from the sidewalks. As she walked, she thought of Alissa and hoped that her sister would be able to shake off her despair and enjoy the holidays. The dramatic mountains were breathtaking, and Jo was sure a day outside surrounded by all this beauty would do Alissa good.

Living in the city, it was never quiet. Jo didn't get the chance to experience much of the outdoors. When the weather was nice, she walked to Grant Park and got in some exercise, but it wasn't the same as all of this wide-open space. As she finished another loop, she watched the pure, unadulterated morning light make its first appearance and glint off the snowy mountain tops. The sunlight made the snow glitter like it was sprinkled with tiny diamonds, and the sight took Jo's breath away.

The lodgers were beginning to waken, with a few of them outside on their way up the mountain already. As Jo made her way back to the main lodge, a fluffy golden retriever came bounding over a pile of snow and slid into her.

She bent down, looked into his gentle brown eyes, and gave the big guy a scratch between his ears. His snout was dusted with snow and tiny snowballs clung to the feathers along his legs and belly. "Where did you come from, sweet boy?" Jo wished she had a dog of her own, but her apartment and her schedule wouldn't allow it.

Seconds later, she heard a deep voice booming, "Finn, Finn, get back here."

Jo glanced at the metal tag on the dog's bright red collar. "I think somebody's looking for you." She swore Finn winked at her.

Jo didn't see Finn's owner, thinking he was on the pathway a level below her, but yelled out, "Finn's over here, near the entrance at the back of the main lodge."

Moments later, a tall guy wearing a knitted cap with the Cedar Mountain Lodge logo came around the corner. "There you are, you clown." He waved a gloved hand at Jo. "Sorry about that. He normally stays right next to me."

Jo almost grinned when she noticed his smiling hazel eyes. And he had a hint of scruff on his cheeks and chin. "It's not a problem. Finn's a sweet guy, I can tell." The dog leaned against Jo's leg.

The man put a hand on the dog's head. "He's never met a stranger." He frowned and squinted his eyes a bit. "Josie? Is that you?"

At the sound of her old nickname, one that only her

grandma and one other person ever used, she studied his eyes. "Luke?"

"I can't believe it," he said, engulfing Jo in a hug, his tough insulated work coat meeting her puffy ski jacket. "I haven't seen you for what, more than fifteen years? I was so sorry to hear of your grandma's passing. She was such a sweet lady. Mom and Dad wrote to me and told me." He kept squeezing her tight.

Jo swallowed the lump in her throat. Luke had always been a good guy, spent a fair amount of time at the library, and was so kind to her and Grandma Maeve. He'd help her with heavy boxes of books and did any jobs around the library that required muscle. He was older than Jo, by about four years, so she only knew him from the time she spent in town. The last time she had seen him was right before Grandma died.

She remembered him being tall, but he was well over six feet now and from the width of his shoulders and the feel of his arms around her, solid and muscular. He smelled like coffee and sawdust.

He released her and smiled. She recognized the kindness she had always seen in his eyes. "Are you just here for the holidays?" She pointed at his hat. "Or, are you working here?"

"I just got back home in November. I'm living at Gina's place. You remember my oldest sister, five years old than me? She's actually watching Maddie's dog for her. Come to think of it, I shouldn't be too surprised to see you here for the wedding. I just hadn't given it much thought."

Jo eyes sparked with recognition. "Yes, yes, I remember Gina from your dad's shop. How are your parents?" And of course, Luke would know about the wedding, especially with his sister watching Maddie's dog. The whole small town of Granite Ridge probably knew. That was the upside of living in a city, nobody knew anything about you, but nobody really cared either.

"Right, growing up we all worked in the shop for a stint. Mom and Dad are doing well. They're spending the holidays in California with my other sisters, Rachel and Lauren and their kids."

"You said you're home now. So are you done with the military?"

He nodded and patted Finn's head. "Yep, I couldn't handle more than sixteen years. It's tough." He knelt down to clip a leash to Finn's collar. "Granite Ridge is where I'll be for the foreseeable future. I'm doing a bit of handyman work here at the lodge. Gina just opened a pet supply place in town, so I'm giving her a hand with that. She convinced me to dip my toe into the dog walking business."

"That's a change of pace, I'm sure." Jo's face was getting colder by the minute. "I'm going to go in and grab a coffee. Care to join me?"

"I would, but I can't. I'm on the clock. How about tonight? There's a big bonfire by the skating rink. Finn and I are going and if you're not too involved with the wedding plans, we could meet up there?" His smile reached all the way to the tiny crinkles at the corner of his eyes, making him impossible to refuse. Add the pleading brown eyes of his beautiful golden sidekick and Jo was powerless.

"I understand if you can't get away…"

Jo grimaced. She might as well tell him; he'd know soon enough anyway. "There aren't any wedding plans. Don't say too much, but it's been called off. We just got the word a couple of days ago, and decided to come and enjoy the lodge anyway."

Luke's smile faded. "I'm sorry to hear that. Maddie was so excited about it. She didn't say anything when she dropped Tumbleweed with Gina."

"It's been stressful and we're all just trying to support Alissa."

Luke glanced across the walkway. "Sorry, I need to get a move on. See you tonight?" Beneath the folded brim of his cap, his eyes widened in question.

"I'll be there," Jo said, bending to ruffle Finn's ears. "Shall we trade cell numbers, and I'll text you if anything changes?" She pulled her phone from her pocket and keyed in his digits, sending him a quick text so he had hers and gave him a wave as he and Finn hurried down the pathway.

Jo had seen the event schedule in her room and posted throughout the lobby. She hadn't planned to go to the bonfire, thinking it best to wait and see what Maddie had organized or if Alissa needed anything, but seeing Luke had intrigued her. She wanted to know more about what had happened in the past fifteen years of his life and Finn's charm was irresistible.

She stomped the snow from her boots and made her way to the huge fire blazing in the lobby. By the time she had warmed her hands and thawed out, it was time to meet everyone for breakfast.

She wandered into the café and spotted her mom. Dressed in a beautiful blouse with shiny beads and sequins decorating it, Maddie rushed from her seat and wrapped her arms around Jo, happy tears shining in her tired eyes. "I'm so glad you're here."

After they ordered their meals, Maddie guided the conversation to Jo, since it had been so long since she'd been home. "How was your office party? Did the blouse we picked out work?"

Jo smiled, taking a sip of tea from her mug. "It wasn't as bad as I thought and the blouse was perfect and I brought it with me. I raked in enough wine, bath products, and high-end snacks to get me through to summer. I think the partners feel guilty for working us so hard all year, so they over compensate at Christmas."

Maddie told them Nan was upstairs resting in their suite after her long travel day yesterday. She had been on a cruise, and then had to make her way across the country with too many delayed connections and canceled flights. Her back was bothering her and she still needed to rest and recharge.

Hailey and Maddie had tried to convince Alissa to come to breakfast, but she just wasn't up to it. It was hard to see Alissa so distraught and they wanted to cheer her up, but weren't sure quite how to do it. The holiday event flyer sparked an idea and soon they had cooked up a plan to convince Alissa to participate in some of the fun happenings going on in the lodge.

In addition to all the outdoor activities that were always available at the lodge, they had a special lineup of holiday fun. Crafts and ornament making, along with gingerbread house building sounded like it would be right up Alissa's alley. She was always coming up with creative things to do with the kids in her classroom.

Between them, they vowed to drag Alissa from the suite and get her involved in something. Jo wanted to change out of her walking clothes and after promising to catch up with them, she dashed upstairs to her suite. After getting ready and looking through her clothes, figuring out what best to wear to the bonfire and skating party, she ventured downstairs.

The inviting smell of coffee beckoned her to stand in line at the coffee counter. While she waited, she took in the bustle of activity and all the smiling faces of the guests, many with children tugging their hands, excited for the Winterfest activities famous at Cedar Mountain.

Jo took her peppermint mocha and settled into one of the

big leather chairs next to the fireplace, relishing the warmth. Glancing across the space, Jo spotted Maddie near the coffee counter, talking to an attractive middle-aged man. Maddie laughed and smiled as the man said something to her. Had she not known better, she could swear he was flirting with Maddie, and she seemed to be welcoming it, smiling with a playful expression. When he turned, Jo saw his shirt had the Cedar Mountain Lodge logo on it and pushed the idea of her mother flirting with a man aside. Maddie was probably just taking care of all the details associated with canceling the wedding.

She caught up with Hailey and Alissa, and they ran into Stevie at the cookie decorating station, showing off her skills. Stevie was explaining to a group gathered around her how to flood the shaped cookies with icing that would need to dry before embellishing them further. Jo edged closer to watch as Stevie took a snowflake cookie, iced with subtle blue frosting that reminded Jo of the silver and blue wintery hues Alissa had chosen for her wedding colors, and began to add white dots and scrolls with tiny piping tips. Then she dusted it with glittering sugar, and within minutes had a gorgeous snowflake that looked more like a piece of art than a sweet dessert.

Jo knew she could never make a cookie that looked that perfect. She caught Stevie's eye and waved, giving her a thumbs up sign, then continued on to the area set up for holiday crafting. She took a chair and a woman dressed in an elf costume got her set up with a small wooden board, stencils, paints, and brushes.

Jo wasn't crafty, but fell in love with a cute wooden porch decoration with a cheerful snowman. Not that she had an actual porch, but if it turned out, she'd give it to Maddie or Hailey. It took time, almost three hours, and when she was done, Jo couldn't help but admire the welcoming snowman on a black background with snowflakes scattered around him. Next, she painted a matching wine-colored scarf and hat band she decorated with white polka dots. The expert helping the crafters showed her how to add in a few subtle curly designs around the scarf that really set it off and made it look professional.

She left it to dry, searched for her sisters or mom, but didn't see anyone, and slipped into the Cedar Mountain Lounge for a quick lunch, checking her phone for any messages. Seeing none, she took a small table showcasing a perfect view from the floor to ceiling windows. The snowy scene led her to order the hearty soup and sandwich special.

On her way back to the craft room, she helped herself to a cookie from the tray in the lobby, recognizing it as one of Stevie's beautiful snowflakes. She did a double-take when she walked by the fireplace and noticed a golden retriever napping on a red and green plaid dog bed at the edge of the hearth. He looked an awful lot like Finn.

She moved closer and recognized the red collar she had seen earlier. She couldn't read the tag without disturbing him, but knew he was Luke's dog. The lodge touted it was pet-friendly, but Finn must have ambassador status to have his own bed in the lobby and be left unattended.

Finn's presence meant Luke had to be nearby. Jo wondered what he did at the lodge. The way he had been dressed, she thought he worked outdoors. She left Finn dozing, picked up her snowman project, and headed back to her room. After fixing a cup of tea, she snuggled into the sofa to watch a Christmas movie.

The actor's smile reminded her of Luke's. She'd had a bit of a school girl crush on him, but hadn't given him much thought after he went off to the military. After losing Grandma Maeve, there was no time for frivolous thoughts about older boys or other fanciful dreams. Her sole focus had been on surviving, and until she met Maddie, she wasn't sure she would succeed.

Most everyone at work was married or dating someone, but Jo hadn't ever met the right guy. She hadn't even gone on a date in months, too busy with work or volunteering with foster children, and not interested in wasting time with the shallow guys she had encountered. A few matchmakers at the office had tried setting her up with friends and relatives, but nothing ever clicked. Jo suspected it was her fault. Patience was not her strong suit and being married wasn't high on her list of goals. She wasn't sure that she could ever truly trust someone enough to be married.

The life she had constructed could get lonely, and she longed for the closeness and companionship of Maddie and her sisters. Being surrounded by that sense of unconditional love and support was something she craved. Her work with foster children helped fill the void, but also reminded her of what she had left behind for her career.

Unlike her, so many children, especially teenagers, ended up aging out while in the foster system. She had been appalled at what she had endured and it was nothing compared to many of the children she encountered. Much of the volunteer work Jo did at Love Links consisted of legal filings and court appearances to represent the interests of foster children and adoptive parents, but her greatest joy came from helping those that were aging out in the system.

She couldn't fathom how an eighteen-year-old was supposed to move out of foster care and support herself without help, much less go to college or find a good job. Jo and the other volunteers, many of whom were involved in radio and television, used their voices to raise funds and administer a non-profit, set up to provide exactly the type of support a young adult without a family needs. A job, housing, transportation, scholarships for college were difficult enough, but without anyone in your corner, they were almost impossible.

Love Links strived to get the older teens adopted, but it

was challenging. With so many of the teens aging out while still in care, the volunteers concluded they couldn't rely on finding adoptive families, so instead worked to establish group homes where teens would have a safe place to live and the support they needed to establish a life of their own. Far too many ended up homeless and jobless, so bridging the gap between foster care and adulthood was among their top missions.

Jo spent much of her time mentoring at the group homes, helping those interested in college to secure scholarships and grants, or helping the others who desired to work to find employment. She'd had the privilege of attending several college graduations and even a couple of weddings of those she had mentored.

Her career provided financial security and a comfortable life, but her volunteer work at Love Links brought her the most satisfaction and true joy. It also made her realize what a rare person Maddie was, to open her heart to not just one, but four foster girls, who without her might have ended up stuck in the system, like so many of the troubled kids Jo met. Her kindness and love knew no bounds and instead of withdrawing after the tragic loss of her husband and little girl, Maddie had healed her wounds by helping others. Her example made a strong impression and lived on in Jo's work.

As the movie flashed across the screen, Jo's mind continued to wander until she nodded off, with the fire glowing nearby and cozy under the warm throw.

A ping from her phone woke her several hours later. Startled, it took her a few seconds to remember she was at the lodge. When she saw the time on her phone, her eyes widened. "Geez, I slept the whole afternoon," she muttered as she scrolled to the message.

She smiled when she saw Luke's name. *I'm done with work and wondered if you'd like to meet for dinner before the bonfire? You name the time and I'll meet you at Jackson's.*

Something fluttered in Jo's chest. Excitement, nervousness, she wasn't sure. Before responding, she checked her messages and saw a group message from Maddie, who included Stevie and Hailey. Maddie let them know Alissa was huddled up in her room and suggested they might want to pop in and cheer her up, but not mention Jed. Maddie was happy to meet anyone who was available for dinner, but wanted the girls to do whatever they wanted. She realized everyone would need some time to rest and recover from the emotional turmoil and travel.

Seeing she had no commitments for dinner, she tapped in a quick reply and said she'd meet Luke at Jackson's around six o'clock. That would give her enough time to stop by Alissa's and check in on her.

Moments later, her phone chimed and she saw a smiling emoji. Jo didn't wear much makeup, and hadn't bothered with any this morning, so she applied her usual minimal look, then went wild and dusted her eyelids with a shimmering gold shadow. The nap had flattened one side of her hair, so she took some time to curl it, using her fingers to style it. Then, knowing it would be cold outside, she chose a thick copper colored sweater woven with metallic threads. Maddie had given it to her last year, telling her the threads matched her hair.

She paired it with her favorite jeans, thicker socks, and warm boots, then searched through her small jewelry box. She frowned at the pearl necklace that she had forgotten to leave home. Maddie had given each of them pearls when they graduated high school, and Alissa wanted them all to wear them for the wedding.

She added a pair of earrings, gathered her puffy coat, gloves, and scarf, and headed down the hall to Alissa's room.

As soon as the door locked, she turned and used her card to open it and grabbed the snowman decoration she had made.

Alissa was still in her pajamas when she answered the door, the dark circles under her eyes broadcasting her lack of sleep.

"Hey, I just wanted to check on you. How are you feeling today?" Jo rested the snowman near the Christmas tree.

Alissa shrugged and went back to her nest on the couch, under the throw blanket. The television was on, but the volume was turned so low, Jo almost couldn't hear it. Containers of comfort food lined the counter and Jo knew Stevie had been by bearing gifts, coaxing Alissa to eat.

Jo pointed at the snowman. "Can you believe I made this today? They've got a great crafting area set up downstairs. You'll have to check it out. If they could help me make this, imagine what you could do with your creative brain?"

Her sister looked at it and smiled. "That's really well done. That would look cute on Mom's porch."

"Yes, I'm going to give it to her or Hailey, since I don't have a porch."

Alissa's eyes traveled over Jo. "You look dressed up. Are you going somewhere tonight?"

"I ran into an old friend this morning, someone who knew my grandma. We're meeting for dinner and then we might check out the skating and bonfire."

Tears pooled in Alissa's eyes. "That sounds fun." She plucked a tissue from the box next to her, wiped her eyes, and added it to the brimming wastebasket. "I'm sorry, I just can't seem to snap out of this funk. I keep wavering between anger and utter despair. Jed was the one for me. I'm not sure how I'm going to go on without him. All our dreams..."

Jo sat down next to her and moved Alissa's legs across her lap, like she used to when Alissa was little. "I'm the last person to give relationship advice. I don't date much and haven't even considered marriage. The only thing I can offer in the way of guidance is not to delegate your happiness to anyone else. You are enough. You're strong. You're loved. You're kind and wonderful and bring joy to others, especially the children in your classroom. Whether you're married to Jed or anyone else, doesn't change those things."

Tears fell from Alissa's eyes as she nodded and reached for Jo's hand.

Jo squeezed it and put her other hand on top of Alissa's. "You've endured worse than this, Alissa. You're stronger than you think and you'll recover from this setback. If you grow weak or tired, you have Mom and the rest of us to help. I think you're brave to offer your heart to someone. It's risky and you didn't hesitate. I admire the way you trust people. I sometimes wish I could do the same."

Alissa wiped her tears away. "At the moment, I'm not sure I'd recommend it, but I appreciate what you're saying. I truly loved Jed. I still love him. That's what makes this so hard. If I hated him, it might be easier."

Jo smiled and said, "Stevie's got that angle covered."

That made Alissa laugh, that out of control style of laugh, combined with crying, that turned into what could only be described as ugly laughing. Really ugly. As the snorts subsided, Jo brushed the bangs from Alissa's forehead. "Don't think too far ahead. Maybe think about taking a shower tomorrow and getting dressed, then doing one activity. It might help get your mind off of all of this. I tell you, those crafts are calling your name."

Alissa took a deep breath. "I'll try, thanks Jo. You're right about me surviving worse. After losing my parents, I never thought I'd have a normal life. Without Maddie, I probably wouldn't have. I'll get through this, too. It's just all so fresh right now and hard to understand."

"Without Maddie, none of us would have made it. I often think of her when I need strength."

"She's been wonderful through all of this. Losing all the

money she spent, listening to me blubber and drone on and on. I'm glad she had the idea for everyone to come here and I promise tomorrow will be better. Like you said, I'll get dressed, do something. Maybe we can all meet up for dinner tomorrow and celebrate that we're all here together." Alissa's dark eyes grew bigger as she smiled at Jo.

Jo hugged Alissa close to her. "That sounds perfect."

Jo left Alissa in somewhat better spirits and went downstairs, wandering through the bustling lobby, full of skiers and guests who had spent the day outside and were now gathered around the huge fireplace. Laughter and conversation filled the air, along with the soft notes of Christmas carols.

Jo made her way outside, passed by the huge tree lit up with thousands of twinkle lights and through the door of Jackson's Public House. Notes from a country song she recognized from her play list drifted through the open door. Jackson's offered live music and most of the featured artists leaned heavily on popular country tunes.

The place was packed and Jo wondered if they'd be able to get a table. The hostess caught Jo's eye as she continued to scan the restaurant. "I'm meeting someone here."

The hostess consulted a list. "Could it be Luke?" Jo nodded. "He's already seated and if you follow me, I'll take you to him."

Jo followed her through the maze of pub tables near the bar, passed by the large dance floor, toward the other side of the building. She saw Luke, sitting at a prime table, which during daylight would offer a stunning view of Cedar Mountain. Tonight, it showcased the glimmering town below and the maple and birch trees with trunks and branches blanketed with tiny white lights.

Luke stood and pulled out Jo's chair for her. "I'm glad you could come. How was your day?"

After placing their orders, she told him about hanging around the lodge and her surprise at having fun making a Christmas craft.

"I want to hear all about your life in Chicago. That must be exciting," Luke said, taking a sip of his beer.

She shrugged and said, "Not really that exciting. I'm a corporate lawyer and spend most of my time at work. I have a small, emphasis on small, apartment not far from work, so I walk most days. Any spare time I have usually gets eaten up by my passion project, a volunteer group called Love Links." She went on to explain their mission of helping foster children.

"I get it. When you know you're making a difference in someone's life and actually see it, it's such a great feeling." Luke slathered butter on the warm sourdough bread one of the waitstaff had delivered to their table.

Jo selected a piece for herself. "It's much more rewarding than my normal work. Like you said, I can see the impact."

"I'm sure their predicament is close to your heart." The light from the candle on the table reflected in his sincere eyes. "Mom wrote to me about Maeve and then you having to go into care. That had to be horrible for you. Mom was so relieved when she learned you were with Mrs. Kirby. Mom and Dad considered trying to get certified to become foster parents when they learned about your situation, but they were worried they were too old. When she found out you were in a safe home, she was so happy."

Jo pondered his words, remembering Maria Turner, Luke's mom, who had worked at the elementary school and was always sweet to Jo. His dad, Ray, owned an auto repair shop, and was the only mechanic Grandma Maeve trusted with her car. They were both hard-working and kind. To know they had been so concerned that they considered becoming foster parents, touched Jo. She felt the sting of tears in her eyes.

"Your mom and dad were always so kind. It was a tough time for me, but I was one of the lucky ones. At the time, I didn't understand that, but Maddie saved me, along with my sisters."

"I'm sure you can relate to the kids you're working with, unlike some of the other volunteers."

She took a small bite of warm buttered bread and nodded. "Once the kids know I was in the foster system, they confide in me. The system has a tendency to make you suspicious and it's hard to trust people. All the people who make promises usually don't keep them and it makes you lose faith. After working with them all these years, reading their files, talking to them, it's just heartbreaking." She sipped her wine and shook her head. "Tell me about what you've been up to the last fifteen years."

Luke sat back in his chair, stretched his long legs out, and smiled. "Hmm, I would describe it as busy and stress filled. I had very little time at home, just trip after trip to the Middle East. I was part of a special operations team, so was in some of the worst of it. I finally decided I'd had enough." His smile faded, and a crease appeared between his eyes. "Some memories are too painful."

Jo shook her head. "I can't imagine it. Thank you isn't enough. It seems like a weak response, but I do appreciate your service and that of all of our military. I couldn't do it and I admire those who can. I'm sure you're happy to be home. Are you planning to stay in Granite Ridge?"

The server delivered their meals and Luke's eyes widened at the steak on his plate, surrounded by roasted veggies and the pride of Idaho – mashed russets. "I've only eaten lunch here. Everything has been delicious, but this looks wonderful." He glanced at Jo's roasted chicken with butternut squash risotto and raised his brows. "I'm usually all about steak, but yours looks pretty good."

Jo inhaled the delicious nutty aroma from the parmesan in the risotto and the lemon and herbs from the honey glazed chicken. "If it's half as good as it smells, it will be wonderful."

They took their first bites and groaned with delight. Luke dipped his head toward Jo. "You asked about my plans. I've had my life dictated to me for the last sixteen years, so I've decided I'm done with plans and am going with the flow. I love it here and being close to Mom and Dad, along with Gina. I don't have a plan to leave, but you never know."

Jo couldn't imagine not having a plan, but understood his life had been regimented ever since he left home. "I miss being with family. I don't come home often because it's so hard to leave."

He frowned. "That's a shame. You should come home more often and then it would be easier to leave because you'd already have your next trip planned." He laughed and tipped his glass in her direction.

Jo couldn't help chuckling at his reasoning. "That's an angle I hadn't considered."

"I learned to enjoy the little moments of happiness these last years. I grabbed onto whatever joy I could find. I missed having a dog, so when I got here, Gina helped me find Finn. I've decided I'm going to live my life like him. Seize the moment and not worry about tomorrow, just pack all the happiness I can into each day. It's part of my no-plan strategy."

"I've missed having a dog too. I can't have one in the apartment and it would be alone way too much."

"Sounds like *you* might be alone way too much." Luke winked at her.

He had a point. Jo took another forkful of the cheesy risotto and let it melt in her mouth.

They chatted throughout the rest of the meal, and after,

they were both too stuffed to consider dessert. Instead, they bundled into their coats and wandered down the pathway to the skating rink and the orange glow from the bonfire that lit up the night sky. "Where's Finn?" Jo asked as they walked. "I saw him earlier snoozing in the lobby."

"The front desk managers spoil him rotten. He's a good boy and loves greeting the guests, so it works out well. Since we did dinner, I left him home with Gina and her two dogs, Otis and Watson. They're both golden retrievers and friendly, like Finn. They have a ball together."

A crowd of skaters was on the ice and Jo shook her head when Luke asked if she was game. "Maybe another time when there aren't so many people. I haven't skated for years and am liable to take out the whole lot of them."

Luke laughed and added, "Yeah, I'm not near as flexible as I used to be and have some old injuries, so don't bounce like I did when I was a kid." He led the way to a couple of empty chairs near the bonfire.

Jo held her gloved hands out in front of her. "That feels great, and it's so pretty with the dark sky."

"It took several hours to stack all the wood up today. They've got more bonfire nights on the calendar, I think. Job security, right?"

"Do you like working here?"

A staff member with a Santa hat walked by and offered them cookies and cocoa. They each took a cup of the warm chocolate topped with marshmallows. "I do. Everyone is nice and it's the type of job you don't have to worry about when you leave. It's usually just a few hours a day. All of my normal dog walking clients are either gone for the holidays or off work and walking their own dogs, so I've been picking up a few extra hours here and there."

"I bet your parents are thrilled you're back home."

Luke's grin widened. "That they are. It's been great. I stop by Rusty's Café each morning and shoot the breeze over coffee and fresh baked pastries. Dad usually comes with me and then I do my morning dogs before heading up here. Normally I'm off in the early afternoon, grab lunch here at the lodge, since it's included for employees, head down and help Gina for a bit, stop by and visit Mom and Dad and either eat dinner with them or Gina. It sounds incredibly boring and small-town, but I love it."

"I loved Rusty and Mabel. I can't believe they still run the cafe."

"We'll have to make a plan to stop in one day. Mabel's pies are still the best I've ever tasted."

"Definitely. I'd love to see them."

"Not sure what your plans are, but I've got to help Gina at the store the day after tomorrow. You could come with me and see her store and we can make a pie run at Rusty's."

"My plans are pretty loose, except for tomorrow. I booked a spa day, in preparation for all the wedding festivities. The rehearsal dinner was scheduled for the twenty-third with the ceremony on Christmas Eve. We're all kind of in a holding pattern, waiting to see how Alissa does. I stopped by and saw her for a few minutes tonight and she seemed in better spirits, so I'm hoping she gets out and about tomorrow. She sounded like she wanted all of us to have dinner tomorrow, so that's a step in the right direction."

"That's a tough one. Rejection is never easy, but getting dumped just a few days before your wedding is a whole new level of misery."

"Sounds like you speak from experience." Jo raised her brows over her cup of cocoa.

"Let's just say my work wasn't conducive to relationships. Most of my connections with women didn't rise to the level of an actual relationship, and those that did were short-lived. It might surprise you, but most women aren't looking for someone who can't tell them where they're going, how long they'll be gone, or what they're doing. Wrap all that up with the fact that you might not come back and it makes for one date wonders. I really don't know how the married guys keep it altogether."

"I'm sure the constant stress wears on a marriage."

Luke finished his cocoa. "I should probably head home and rescue Gina from the three dogs. They all think they're furry humans, not to mention spoiled rotten. And Gina has been a little down without her girls here for the holidays." He offered Jo a hand up and she took it.

They took the long way back to the lodge, enjoying the warm lights tucked into every shrub and bush along the way. They entered the lodge through the back entrance, where she had met Finn. Despite the late hour, the lobby was filled with people crowded around the fireplace, drinking and visiting.

They reached the staircase and Jo turned to Luke, smiling. "You don't need to walk me to my door."

"My father would insist on it. He taught me that a gentleman always escorts a lady to her door." He offered her his arm and she slipped hers into his.

They reached her door and she turned and met his eyes. Noticing, not for the first time, their tendency to change color based on whatever Luke was wearing. Tonight, the olive Henley he wore brought out the green in them. He leaned closer and hugged her. The stubble on his cheeks brushed against hers and sent a tingle through her entire body. She breathed in the scent of his hair, a mixture of citrus with a hint of woodsmoke. "Enjoy your spa day tomorrow, and let me know if it works out to run down to town the next day."

"I will, that sounds fun."

"Sweet dreams, Jo," he said, squeezing her hand before turning and making his way down the hallway. She was still standing at her door, watching him, savoring the warmth from his hand that lingered on hers, when he paused at the staircase, looked back, and waved. Her pulse quickened, and suddenly, she felt exposed, like he would see the effect he had on her. With clumsy fingers, she unlocked her door and without looking his way again, slipped over the threshold, shut the door behind her, and leaned there, eyes closed.

This wasn't the time. Alissa didn't need to be reminded of her loss. And it wasn't practical; Luke lived here and she didn't. So while she could enjoy Luke's company as an old friend, that was as far as she could go – no matter what her body seemed to be telling her.

CHAPTER 5

After breakfast in her room, Jo spent several hours at the spa, relaxing with a facial and massage before a pedicure and manicure, followed by having her hair styled. Since the wedding was off, none of it was necessary, but she had been looking forward to a day of pampering. Despite all the access to spas in Chicago, it was something she never did for herself. She was lucky to squeeze in a haircut every couple of months.

By mid-afternoon, her day of beauty was complete. Feeling rejuvenated, she and her shiny plum colored toes, made their way back to her suite. She had left her cell phone behind, not wanting to worry about forgetting it, and with one glance she knew something had happened.

She had dozens of messages and missed call alerts. Her eyes widened and she gasped as she sat by the fire and scrolled through them. Jed had shown up at the lodge to surprise Alissa and the wedding was back on, as was the rehearsal dinner.

Things were already in motion with Maddie talking to the wedding coordinator at the lodge about reviving the ceremony and reception. How she expected to get everything ready in the next forty-eight hours was a mystery.

Jo leaned her head back and sighed. The muscles that had been loosened with massage, were already tightening. "Why didn't I just bring the blasted dress?" She would never find a bridesmaid dress now. She kept reading the messages. Months before, Maddie had engaged a local seamstress, who worked out of a small clothing shop in Granite Ridge, to do the fittings for Stevie and Hailey. She suggested Jo contact Mrs. Lott at the shop, since the bridal store in Boise had previously sent two sample dresses for Stevie and Hailey to try. Maddie hoped they might still have them there.

Jed, via Alissa, had extended a dinner invitation to her family for tomorrow night. He wanted to treat them all to something special and apologize for the chaos he had caused. Jo checked the time and realized she needed to get to work on locating a suitable dress. Luckily, Alissa had chosen a variety of dresses, all in shades of subtle blues, silvers, and grays. All of the sisters had chosen different colors and styles, so she wouldn't have to match anyone exactly. She could run into Boise tomorrow if she struck out at the boutique, but that would make for a harried day.

After throwing on some clothes, Jo tapped in a quick text to her mom and sisters, letting Alissa know how happy she was for her. She didn't dare question her sister's judgment, but wondered to herself how she was able to forgive him so quickly. She let Alissa know that she would be on the hunt for a dress and meet up with everyone later.

Jo made quick work of the mountain roads and parked on Main Street. She walked by Wags and Whiskers, the new store Luke's sister had opened, but didn't have time to stop in and say hello. She was on a mission.

The seamstress, Mrs. Lott, occupied an alcove in the back of the store. Jo hurried through the racks of clothes and breathed a sigh of relief when she found the woman at her sewing machine. The tiny room was crammed with fabric, boxes, and racks of clothes under protective plastic cases. Jo couldn't fathom how Mrs. Lott got any work done in such a cramped workspace.

The petite woman lifted her head, her jet-black hair at odds with the deep wrinkles in her face and the age spots covering her hands. "Mrs. Lott?" Jo asked, tapping her phone to bring up the information about the dress styles Alissa had chosen months ago.

"Yes, dear. How can I help you?"

"My mother, Maddie Kirby, sent me to see if by any chance you still had the sample bridesmaid dresses my sisters tried on?" Jo turned the phone toward the woman.

She frowned and eyed the photo. "Oh, yes, such beautiful dresses." She turned her head and scanned the four corners of the room. "I don't remember sending them back. Let me think."

Jo took a deep breath and resisted the urge to start tearing into all the stacks of haphazard boxes. To say Mrs. Lott moved at a snail's pace would be an insult to snails everywhere. She watched the tiny woman's hands shake as she touched each box. Jo got the feeling she was making the woman nervous. "I'm going to look around the store and I'll check back with you in a few minutes."

Jo scanned a few of the racks, while she pondered solutions to her dress problem, realizing she needed to find some things in addition to the bridesmaid dress. Although she had brought her fancy green blouse for the New Year's Eve party at the lodge, and planned to wear her work pants with it, she wondered if pairing it with a skirt might be better for that event. She rifled through a few racks and saw a long black velvet skirt that might do the trick. Now what she really needed was something casual for the rehearsal dinner. She knew the original plan involved a barbeque and beer themed event, but Jo wasn't sure if jeans would be a little too casual.

There was a holiday display of glittery and sequined dresses and tops that caught Jo's eye. The woman who had been behind the counter when Jo arrived, approached her. "Is there something I can help you find?"

Jo gave her a brief explanation of her need for a rehearsal dinner outfit and explained about Alissa's on-again wedding and her search for a bridesmaid's dress with Mrs. Lott. "Oh, you must be Jo, right? I'm Kathy, the owner here. I met your mom, Maddie, when she was in to coordinate the fittings. Did Mrs. Lott find the dresses?"

Jo's forehead creased. "She was looking and said she didn't remember sending them back."

"Oh, dear. She probably forgot. I decided to keep them and have a small selection of styles here in town for wedding parties up at the lodge. We often run into women looking for something suitable at the last minute. I was even toying with the idea of renting some of them for wedding parties. I just haven't had time to work on getting them organized, and they're still stored in the back room. Give me a second, and we'll see if we can get you set up with something that will work." She plucked two shimmering tops from the rack, a blazer with a waterfall hem, and matching pants in a soft leather looking material. "Try these on and see what you think. It would be a perfect choice for a casual rehearsal dinner, but a little dressier than jeans. I'll bring you the dresses in a jiffy."

With wide eyes, Jo took the hangers from her. "I can't tell you how thankful I am that you kept those dresses."

"I got a great deal on them. I convinced the bridal shop owner down in Boise to partner with me. We're going to bring in several samples after the first of the year and gear up for wedding season. I'll let Mrs. Lott know she can call off the search."

Jo tried the silvery blouse with the black skirt, which looked nice, but not amazing. Although she would have never picked the pants and blazer, she loved how they looked with the glittery golden copper blouse. She knew Maddie had a pair of fancier black ankle boots that would work with the pants, if the open toe sandals she wore to the office party didn't look right. While she was taking another look in the mirror, Kathy's voice came from the other side of the door. "Come on out and let me see how you look in those."

Jo opened the door and stepped to the floor length mirror opposite the two dressing rooms.

"Wowza, that looks terrific. That color looks great with your gorgeous hair. How do you get it so shiny and beautiful?"

Jo laughed and said, "Courtesy of the spa up at the lodge. I had a deep conditioning treatment and then they styled it today."

"Well, it's lovely." She held up four dress bags. "Found these, so you can try them and see if we have something that is a close fit for you. We also have a few shoes, but I'm not sure if they'll fit."

Jo and Maddie wore the same size in shoes, so she had planned to raid her mother's closet for something that might work. Maddie was a bit of a fashionista, and Jo was sure she'd have something that would match the gown. Jo unzipped the dress bags and checked the sizes. There were two distinct possibilities. Neither was the style she had chosen for herself, but she couldn't be picky. The one that looked the best was a dusty blue chiffon dress in a V-neck, with some light beading on the bodice and a few of the shiny embellishments dripping onto the top of the skirt. It fit the best around the bodice and the A-line skirt camouflaged a few flaws on her lower body.

She came out of the dressing room and found Mrs. Lott waiting with her tape measure and pin cushion. Kathy's eyes widened when Jo turned for her. "That looks like a pretty close fit and is a beautiful gown." She handed Jo a box of shoes, glittery pumps in a silvery gray.

Jo slipped them on and nodded. "I think they'll work, especially for the short amount of time I'll need to wear them. In reality, I don't think they're any worse than the ones I bought. Heels aren't my thing."

Mrs. Lott was already pinning bits of fabric around Jo's shoulders.

"Wonderful," said Kathy. "We'll get this altered a bit for you and you can pick it up tomorrow. Will that work?"

"Yes, and thank you both for the help. I wasn't sure what I was going to do. You are lifesavers."

After a few more turns and pins, Mrs. Lott pronounced her done. On her way back to the dressing room, Jo spied a burgundy poncho with an asymmetrical hem hanging on the wall, paired with jeans and a plain shirt. It looked warm and comfortable. She added it to the collection in her dressing room.

Jo slipped out of the gown, and back into her jeans, adding the chic poncho to the outfit. She smiled at her image, liking the style. She added it to the skirt, her rehearsal dinner outfit and shoes, and toted it all to the counter. Kathy wrote up the purchases and then looked up from her invoice pad. "How about we make a deal? When you get home, just send me the dress you bought and the shoes and we can make an even trade. I hate to have you buy two dresses, and can use what you bought as easily as what you're taking today."

Jo's eyebrows arched with surprise. "That's so kind of you, and unexpected. Are you sure?"

Kathy smiled. "Of course, it's no problem and I'm happy to help." She gave Jo a business card with her mailing address and added her cell phone to the back of it. "If you have any issues, just give me a call and we'll work it out."

Jo slid her credit card across the counter, noting the amount was much less than she anticipated. She looked at the invoice and saw Kathy had applied a twenty-five percent discount.

Kathy smiled at Jo's obvious surprise, and pointed to the front window where a huge sign advertised a sale.

"Wow, it is really my lucky day," said Jo. "I hope some of that luck rubs off on Mom and her work to get things organized at the lodge." She gave Kathy her contact information and added, "I'll be home the first week in January and will ship them right out to you. I truly appreciate the offer, not to mention helping me find all this. I'm not usually much of a shopper."

"You'll be comfortable, warm, and gorgeous for the dinner. I love that poncho you picked, it's the perfect winter piece." Kathy hung the blazer and covered it in plastic, then wrapped Jo's purchases in tissue before placing them in a heavy shopping bag. "Have a wonderful Christmas and wedding. Be sure to tell your mom hello, and we'll see you tomorrow."

Jo thanked her again and carried her collection out the door. As she was making her way back to the Jeep, Luke popped out of the door of Wags and Whiskers. "Hey, what are you doing with all that?"

Jo smiled and shook her head. "It's a long story."

"Do you have time for a coffee and to say hello to Gina?" He took hold of her bag and hanger. "I can help you put all this in your car."

His hand brushed against hers as he took hold of the clothes and a thrilling shiver traveled all the way to her toes. Jo consulted her watch and nodded. "I can spare some time."

"Perfect. Gina has one of those fancy coffee makers and a bunch of pods back at the shop."

Jo led the way to her car, then they turned back to Wags and Whiskers. Luke opened the door to the charming shop, decorated with paw prints on the walls. Maddie's dog, Tumbleweed, Finn, and two other goldens rushed toward them, tongues hanging out, begging to be petted. A woman with smiling blue eyes and dark hair pulled back into a no-

nonsense ponytail greeted her. "Hi, Jo, it's nice to see you again. I have fond memories of your grandma, both at the library and Dad's shop."

Jo petted all four dogs while she noted Gina's flawless skin and heart-shaped face. She recognized her from going to Ray's shop with her grandma and seeing her behind the counter with Maria. Gina was about ten years older than Jo, so she didn't have many other memories of her. "Nice to see you, Gina. Your shop is so cute. Luke tells me you opened not long ago."

Gina slipped her arm around her brother's shoulders. "Yes, he's been a big help. Without him, I'd still be trying to get set up."

Luke pulled away and disappeared into a room behind the counter, returning moments later with three steaming mugs. "I've got tea, cocoa, and coffee. Ladies, first," he said, glancing at Jo.

She chose the tea and felt herself relax for the first time since hearing the news about the wedding plans.

"Looks like you found some things over at Kathy's boutique," said Gina, selecting the coffee.

Jo widened her eyes as she explained the situation with the wedding being back on, and having to find a replacement dress for the ceremony as well as something for the rehearsal dinner. "I also found the cutest poncho." She went on to explain how nice Kathy was about taking the original dress and shoes in trade.

Gina sipped on her coffee and nodded. "I'm not surprised. Kathy's as sweet as they come. She opened the boutique just last year, but it seems like she's been here forever."

"I've forgotten what it's like to live in a small town, where there's that inherent trust in neighbors." Jo bent to pet Finn who was leaning rather heavily against her leg.

Luke shook his head. "I'm still trying to process the

wedding news. I bet Maddie is happy. I know how much she was looking forward to it."

"Honestly, I haven't had a chance to talk to anyone. I spent my morning at the spa, totally clueless, and since I got the news, I've been running. But it is the season for miracles." Jo laughed and finished her tea.

"Well, your hair looks gorgeous, so I'd say it was a day well spent." Gina gestured to the glossy waves framing Jo's face.

The door chimed as a customer came into the store, and Gina excused herself. Luke met Jo's eyes. "Your hair does look great." He ruffled the top of Gina's dog, Watson's head. "So, it sounds like you're coming to town to pick up the dress tomorrow. Do you still want to have pie at Rusty's or will you be too busy?"

"Let's plan on it and if things change, I'll let you know."

"Sounds good. I'll be at the lodge in the morning and will catch up with you there."

"I better get a move on and check on everyone. Tomorrow's dinner could prove interesting with what Jed has put everyone through these past few days."

"Make sure and keep the knives away from Stevie." Luke chuckled at his joke. Jo left laughing, but on her drive to the lodge decided she would make a point of sitting next to Stevie tomorrow night. She knew Stevie would be frazzled trying to get another cake made, not to mention skeptical about the wisdom of Alissa's decision to take Jed back and get married like nothing had happened.

A tired, protective Stevie was even more volatile than a regular Stevie.

CHAPTER 6

After staying up late worrying about Alissa and her rush to take Jed back and flip the switch on the wedding, Jo slept in much later than usual. She woke to a text message from Luke, featuring a photo with him and Finn wishing her a good morning, which made her smile. That grin of his was something she hadn't realized how much she had missed.

Under a steamy shower, Jo breathed in the scent of orange blossoms from the shower gel and let her mind wander to Luke. She was looking forward to spending time with him today, visiting Rusty and Mabel, and her famous huckleberry pie, of course. The little tingles of excitement that coursed through her when she was around Luke, were new and unexpected.

There was something about him, something she couldn't quite describe, but it was something that had been missing in other men she had met. It was clear he loved his family; Jo saw that when she visited with him at Gina's shop, and heard it in his voice when he talked about his parents.

He was kind, loved his dog, and had such an easy-going way about him. There were no pretenses, he was genuine –

that was it, that's what she hadn't sensed in the men she had dated in Chicago. It seemed they were all trying too hard, or not trying at all.

After working on her hair and trying to reproduce the subtle waves the stylist had termed beach waves, Jo knew she was going to buy some of the conditioning treatment they had used. Her hair had never looked so healthy. Jo got dressed, choosing one of her favorite sweaters, a deep green one with a loose turtle neck. She was craving a latte, and once ready made her way downstairs to the coffee bar.

When she stepped up to the counter, she was shocked to see Luke behind it, wearing an apron. He smiled and said, "I was just going to text you and see when you'd be ready to head into town. I get off here in a few minutes."

"I didn't know you were also a barista." Jo's eyebrows arched above her playful eyes.

He wiggled his brows at her. "I have many secret talents." He pushed some buttons on the brewer behind him before returning his attention to her. "I just help out wherever they need me. I was here early today and somebody called in sick, so they put me on coffee duty. What can I get you?"

Jo ordered her drink and looked across the lobby. "Is Finn here?" She squinted and stared as she noticed Maddie talking to the same tall man she had seen her with that first morning at the lodge.

Luke was busy steaming milk and gestured with his head toward the front desk. "Finn's in the back, sprawled out napping, I'm sure. He romped around outside early this morning, rolled in the snow, and wore himself out so he earned a rest."

He returned with her drink and swiped her room key to charge it to her account. The little spark of electricity she felt when he gave her the card back and let his fingers linger against her hand wasn't lost on her.

She slipped the card into her purse and pointed across

the space to where Maddie stood with the man in front of the floor to ceiling windows, the sunlight splashing on them. "Do you know who that is? The guy talking to Maddie?"

Luke glanced and nodded. "Oh, yeah, that's Robert, the general manager of the resort. He took over not too long ago."

Jo continued to watch them. Maddie wore one of her favorite outfits in shades of teal green. They both held cups, and she knew Maddie would be drinking tea. The way they leaned into one another suggested he was interested in more than just the wedding plans. Maddie's laugh echoed through the lobby, which made Jo smile. She missed hearing that sound and the comfort it always provided.

"What do you know about him?" asked Jo.

Luke shrugged. "Not much, he's a nice guy and a good boss. Most of the employees like him and he's a stickler for excellent customer service. He has high expectations and can be demanding, but he's a hard worker. I know everybody was a little leery when he came aboard, afraid he might change it and make it too fancy, but he's focused on improvements that were needed and maintenance items that had been neglected."

Jo took a sip and nodded, noting the impressive latte art he had added – a festive snowman. "Aww, love the artwork and it's an excellent latte."

He grinned and said, "Was there ever a doubt?" He nodded to the next customer in line and finished his order before returning to where Jo stood at the end of the counter. "Shall we head into town? Just give me about fifteen minutes to wrap things up here."

"Let me check in with Mom and tell her where I'll be and see if she needs anything from town."

Jo wandered across the lobby and came up behind Robert. When Maddie saw Jo, her eyes went wide. She reached for her daughter's hand and said, "Jo, I'd like you to meet Robert

69

Jeffries, the general manager here. This is my eldest daughter, Jo."

Jo took in his friendly smile and the slight graying at his temples, which added to his distinguished look.

"Wonderful to meet you, Jo. I've heard so much about you." His eyes moved upward in thought. "If I remember correctly, Maddie said you're a successful attorney in Chicago. That must be quite exciting."

"Not nearly as exciting as putting a wedding together in less than two days." Jo chuckled and glanced at her mother. "I ran into Luke. I know him from all the time he spent at the library when my grandma ran it. We're going to Granite Ridge to pick up my dress and stop by Rusty's to say hello. Do you need anything or need me to do anything to help?"

Maddie's grin deepened as she looked up at Robert. "I think everything is in motion. Robert and his staff have gone over and above to make all of this happen." Maddie's eyes turned to meet Jo's. "I'm hoping Stevie can rescue the rehearsal dinner. She's got the cake under control. Hailey is working with Nick on the music. You remember Hensley's Sweet Shop? Nick's sister, Stacy took that over when their mother died, and he's come back to help her. He's a guitarist in a local band and handles most of the music for events up here at the lodge."

"I remember the candy store, but not sure I remember Nick. Maybe when I see him, I will. Sounds like everything is under control. Text me if you need anything. I'll have my cell phone."

"Do you mind stopping by Gina's store and checking on Tumbleweed? You could give him some loving while you're in town. She and Luke are both wonderful, but I always feel guilty leaving him."

Robert bobbed his head in agreement. "Luke's terrific. I wish I had about five of him working for me. He can do anything, fix anything, and has a great attitude. Not to mention, Finn is quite popular with all the guests. He's like our official greeter. Everyone loves both of them."

Jo said goodbye, fetched her coat and gloves from her room, and met Luke and Finn coming from the front desk. "Are you ready?" he asked. Finn's tail thwacked against Jo's legs.

"All set. I'll follow you in my car," she said, heading for the parking area.

"We can take my truck. I don't mind bringing you back. I need to check and see if they need me to work tomorrow anyway."

The day was cold, but the sun was shining, making it a beautiful morning for a drive down the mountain. Jo followed Luke to the shiny red truck she remembered him driving as a teenager. "I can't believe you still have this truck."

He clutched a hand to his chest. "I'd never sell it. My dad restored it and gave it to me for my sixteenth birthday. It's much more than a truck." Luke ran his fingers along the fender of the 1967 Chevy and opened the passenger door. Finn jumped in and Luke made him move over to the middle of the seat.

Jo stepped into the truck, breathing in the scents of citrus, spice, and wood. Except for a few golden dog hairs, the interior was as shiny and clean as the exterior.

"Gina's got a delivery arriving today, so I need to help her stock the heavy bags of dog food. She's going to text me when it arrives. It's a little unpredictable this time of year. Are you up for a late breakfast at Rusty's?"

"Sounds perfect. I'm just now starting to get a little hungry. I won't have to worry about having lunch and can wait until Jed's dinner tonight."

"Right, that should be…interesting?"

She chuckled. "Awkward, is more like it. I'm worried that Alissa may be acting too quickly. Forgiving him, like that."

She snapped her fingers. "I'm sure the whole thing is related to his parents. They refused to be part of the wedding at all, and his mother is horrid." Jo sighed and added, "I'm not sure I could marry someone knowing their family hated me."

Luke grimaced as he slowed his speed on their approach into downtown Granite Ridge. "That's a tough spot Jed's in. Hopefully, things work out. I guess it's proof that money doesn't solve everything, huh?"

Jo nodded as she considered his words. She had always viewed money as a means to a secure future and a solution to never having to rely on anyone, but Luke was right, it didn't guarantee happiness.

He pulled in front of Rusty's Café, and Finn barreled out of the truck as soon as Luke vacated his seat.

Rusty hollered out a hello as they came through the door and pointed to the last booth along the front of the café. Luke led the way and Finn settled in, lying down next to him, against the wall.

A few minutes later, Rusty came from behind the counter and placed a bowl of fresh water on the floor, next to Finn, slipping him a dog biscuit. "Fresh from the oven this morning, Finn. Pumpkin, your favorite." He petted the dog's head.

Luke caught his eye and gestured across the table to Jo. "You remember Jo?"

Rusty's eyes twinkled and a smile filled his face. "Of course, how are you, Jo? It's been a long time since we've seen you. Wonderful to have you back home. I've got to get Mabel out of the kitchen so she can say hello. What can I get you kids this morning?"

Jo never had much time when she visited home, so had missed seeing Rusty and Mabel for several years. He had the same jovial attitude, joking with all the customers, but looked a bit older, his hair thinner and his midsection thicker. "Are you waiting tables now, Rusty? I thought we had to order at the counter?" asked Jo.

"I only wait on special customers, like you." He winked and glanced at the door opening and two people approaching the counter. "I could just tell Mabel to make up something for you, if you trust her."

Jo laughed and nodded her head. "That sounds perfect. Whatever it is, I need a piece of her huckleberry pie, if she has any."

"You got it. She freezes gallons of them when they're in season to make sure she can keep making pies all year."

As Rusty walked away, Luke turned his coffee mug upright, and gave Jo a questioning look.

"I think I'll just do water this morning."

Luke nodded as he rose. He retrieved a pot of coffee from the machine behind the counter, poured himself a cup, and made the rounds at all the booths, filling and freshening cups as he went.

When he returned to the table, he brought Jo a glass of iced water. Jo took in the worn Formica topped table and the counter with the old swivel stools that looked the same, except she was sure they had been reupholstered. "This place, it's like stepping back into time."

He took a long swallow from his cup. "I was so glad it stayed the same. Just like when I left it." He winked and added, "Except for the new fabric on the stools. Actually, the whole town feels like it did when I was a kid. That's part of the charm, the draw of it for me."

Rusty returned with a plate bearing a fresh cinnamon roll, dripping with cream cheese frosting. "Mabel sent this out for an appetizer."

Using his fork, Luke cut out a fat wedge. "Best cinnamon rolls in the world," he said, closing his eyes and swallowing the first bite.

"I'm not sure how I'm going to eat this, breakfast, and a piece of pie." Jo laughed as she cut off a sliver of the pastry and bit into it. "Oh, that is so good. I'd forgotten how delicious they are."

Jo limited herself to one more thin slice of the fluffy cinnamon roll, and Luke gladly took care of the rest. As he finished, Mabel came from behind the counter, carrying their plates. "Jo, I'm so glad to see you, sweetie." She set the plates on the table and reached over to hug Jo. Mabel's hair, which had been streaked with gray the last time Jo saw her, was now completely silver, but styled in a flattering wispy cut. Her face held a few more wrinkles, but her bright blue eyes were the same, full of kindness and love.

Mabel slid into the booth next to Jo and put her arm around her. "I can't believe this is the same little girl who used to sit in here for hours reading and nibbling on pie. You're even more beautiful than the last time we saw you, and such a successful woman. Maddie keeps us up to date on your big-city life. Your grandma would be so proud of you."

Mabel glanced across the table at Luke. "And, we're thrilled Luke is back in Granite Ridge. We love visiting with him each morning, and watching him and Gina open her new business. It's so exciting to have some of our favorite kids all grown up and doing such wonderful things."

Luke smiled. "There's no place I'd rather be. I think I missed your cinnamon rolls more than anything else while I was gone."

Mabel beamed with pride and then turned at the sound of Rusty yelling for her help in the kitchen. "I better get back there before he burns the place down, but wanted to say hello. Enjoy breakfast." She started to leave but then turned and winked at Jo. "I boxed up a huckleberry pie for you, on the house. I'll leave it at the register."

She was gone before Jo could say anything. "Ah, I've missed this."

Luke added salt and pepper to his bacon scramble. "There is truly no place like home. I came here to regroup, after being gone for so long. Just needed a soft place to be, to think, figure out what's next. Now, after being here I'm not sure I can ever bring myself to leave."

"It's not too small for you?"

He shook his head as he finished another bite. "Nah, I like that it feels like a big family. If you need help, someone's always there. I've come to appreciate time with my parents and Gina. I love the outdoors and there's no place more beautiful. It's only a couple hours away from Boise and the airport, if I need a taste of a bigger city."

Jo was surprised at Luke's revelation. Most single people in their thirties weren't looking for a tiny place like Granite Ridge, where sometimes it felt like Main Street rolled up the sidewalks at six o'clock and everyone knew everything about their neighbors. But the value of community wasn't lost on her. She had very few people she could rely on in Chicago. Some work friends, a couple of the volunteers at Love Links, and Doris made up her social circle.

She missed having a place like Rusty's, where she felt comfortable to hang out, whether eating or not. She loved the little café by her apartment, but only for the food and service. It wasn't a place that invited customers to whittle away hours reading a book. Who was she kidding? With her schedule, she didn't have time to waste reading anyway.

Jo insisted on treating Luke to breakfast, though it took some persuasion on her part and reminding him that he picked up the dinner tab at Jackson's. They said their goodbyes to Rusty and Mabel, and after stashing the pie in the truck, strolled down the street to Wags and Whiskers. They found Gina waiting on a customer, and the dogs resting on their beds.

Jo knelt beside the dogs and made sure she gave each one some attention, delivering her mom's message to Tumbleweed. While she was busy with them, she saw Luke head through the rear door that opened into the alley, then heard the airbrakes on a delivery truck and the noise of the liftgate.

The dogs were curious, but not enough to abandon Jo, who was rubbing their ears and chins. She kept them occupied and out of the way, while Gina rang up some tourists who needed food and toys for their dogs.

As soon as she finished with the sale, Gina went through the back door and joined Luke. Between the two of them they carried in the heavy bags of dog food and other supplies that the driver had left on two pallets. Jo offered to help, but they both insisted she stay put and keep the dogs occupied. The last thing they needed was a pack of furry helpers.

With the chilly air coming in through the back door, Jo was thankful to be in the midst of the dogs and their body heat. She used some treats Gina had given her to elicit some tricks from her charges. As she suspected, the goldens all performed on command. Tumbleweed was another story. He wasn't nearly as well trained as his friends and tended to march to his own beat.

As soon as they finished carting in all the supplies and stocking the shelves, Luke secured the door and Jo untangled herself from the furry masses. "I'm going to run next door and pick up the dress, if it's ready."

Luke rubbed his hands together and put a coffee pod in the brewer. "I'll be here and can run you back up to the lodge whenever it works."

First, Jo stopped by the florist and picked up a small bouquet of red and white flowers. At the dress shop, Kathy greeted Jo with a smile, and reached for the gown that hung on the rack next to the counter. "You can slip this on and make sure it works. Mrs. Lott is still here in case she needs to adjust anything."

Jo followed Kathy and detoured to Mrs. Lott's sewing area, finding her bent over her machine. "I wanted to thank you for your kindness and doing the alterations to my dress so quickly. I really appreciate you making it a priority."

Mrs. Lott's eyes brightened as her smile widened. "Oh, you didn't need to do that. It was easy, not much to it, really."

"Well, I appreciate it nonetheless. I hope you enjoy the flowers." Jo handed her the square vase.

"They're the perfect addition to my Christmas table. Thank you, dear."

Jo hurried to the dressing room, freezing as she took off her warm sweater and realized she left her coat at Gina's shop. Shivering, she slipped into the sleeveless gown, thankful she had packed the faux fur wrap, since she would definitely need it. Jo admired the dress and thought it looked fine, but Kathy made her come out so she could inspect it.

Both Kathy and Mrs. Lott checked her shoulders and waist, making sure the dress didn't gap and wasn't too snug. They both gave their nods of approval and as Jo turned to go back to the dressing room, Luke walked through the door.

He saw her and stopped, holding her coat in front of him, his eyes wide. "Wow, you're uh, well…gorgeous."

Jo's cheeks flushed as she stood before him.

He shook her coat and said, "I noticed you left it at the store and just wanted to bring it to you."

"Thanks, I'll be back in just a few minutes." She hurried past him and into the dressing room. She heard Kathy exchange pleasantries with Luke as she carefully removed the gown and hung it back on the hanger. A quick glance in the mirror confirmed what she already knew. Her neck and face were beet red with embarrassment. She strained to listen and didn't hear his voice, willing herself to relax and take deep breaths. Seeing him had flustered her. Why had it made her feel so vulnerable?

She wasn't used to compliments related to her appearance. Praise for her work, and gratitude for helping at Love Links were normal everyday occurrences, but flattery related to her beauty was foreign. She didn't trust the words. Jo didn't consider herself attractive, didn't concentrate on makeup or fashion, and usually the compliments related to either were from people looking for favors, or who simply expected pleasantries.

She rubbed the still lumpy scar near her left thumb. It was a reminder of what she was willing to do to escape the horrible foster family situation she had been in before finding Maddie. There, she had healed, flourished after time, and found a family. Maddie and Nan had always told Jo she was beautiful, but even if they meant it, it wasn't the same as hearing it from a handsome man like Luke. A man, who without saying a word, could make Jo's pulse quicken.

As she stood in the dressing room, she contemplated her immediate reaction to what was by all accounts a sincere and spontaneous compliment from Luke. She knew Luke was kind and authentic, and sighed as it dawned on her that she was making way too much of it. Why couldn't she just smile and say thank you instead of acting so embarrassed?

Grandma Maeve had raised only Jo's dad and hadn't had any little girls in her life until Jo came along. Instead of lavishing her with fancy clothes and toys, she had put her efforts into Jo's intellect, making sure she was exposed to books, conversations, and ideas. In addition to devouring books, they attended city and county meetings, even went to the legislature in Boise a few times, and saw almost every movie that played in Granite Ridge. Grandma Maeve had loved movies and shared her fondness for them with Jo.

She had also passed on her strong work ethic and integrity, raising Jo to be honest and principled with little to no emphasis on outward beauty. Jo never remembered Grandma Maeve wearing anything but her no nonsense pants and blouses with a cardigan. She didn't wear makeup, and only occasionally wore simple earrings, and despite being a widow, always wore her wedding ring.

Living with Maddie had opened a whole new world to Jo. Maddie loved gorgeous clothes and jewelry, had a closet full of shoes, and basketfuls of skincare and beauty products in her bathroom. The only piece of jewelry Jo wore each day was the delicate sterling Celtic knot ring Grandma Maeve had given her shortly before she passed.

Jo was hopeless when it came to accessorizing or pairing outfits together, but Maddie was a master. Alissa and Hailey, being much younger, grew up with her influences and with what seemed like little effort always looked polished and beautiful.

Stevie and Jo were more alike and older, neither of them coming from places where fashion and beauty took center-stage. Although Jo thought Stevie's auburn hair was unique and fit her, Stevie never liked it and compared it to the color of carrots. While Jo took very little pains with her appearance, Stevie took even less. Jo couldn't remember seeing her in anything other than the shapeless jeans and hooded sweat-shirts she favored when she wasn't wearing chef's clothes. Her hair was usually pulled back or in a bun, due to her work in the kitchen.

Maddie's sense of grace and style hadn't rubbed off on either one of them, which is why Jo relied on her for long distance shopping advice. Maddie had promised to help Jo and Stevie dress for the wedding and the rehearsal dinner, and could be counted on to bring tons of jewelry and acces-sories to make sure they had the right pieces, to make their outfits 'pop', as she was fond of saying.

Jo collected the dress, thanked Kathy again, and made her way back to Gina's shop. Luke and Finn were ready to go when she came through the door. He took the dress and carried it down the street to his truck, making sure the dress was placed with care across Jo's lap once she was seated.

He let Finn enter through the driver's door and kept him

close. Finn spent the ride with his nose in the air, undoubtedly smelling the pie in the box at Jo's feet.

On the ride up to the lodge, they chatted about Christmas plans. Luke and Gina had decided to splurge on Christmas Eve dinner at the lodge this year, since it was just the two of them. Gina was cooking for Christmas Day, making all of their favorites. As Luke made the turn off the highway, he glanced over at Jo. "In fact, Gina wanted me to be sure to invite you to join us Christmas Day. If you're not doing anything, come by around three o'clock or whenever it works."

Jo petted Finn with her free hand, while she held onto the dress with the other. "That's so nice of her, of both of you. From what I know, I think I'll be free. We're having Christmas brunch together, but nothing planned after that. I'm sure everyone will be tired from the festivities and happy to relax."

He explained where Gina's house was, which was just a few blocks from Maddie's. "We'll plan on you being there and if it doesn't end up working out, just text me." He pulled into the parking lot and added, "It's casual, so wear whatever. We're not going fancy and you'll have four dogs who'll want to snuggle with you."

"Sounds perfect. I like casual. I rarely dress up, so all of this fuss is strange, but I'm trying to go with the flow."

Luke unloaded Finn, then took charge of the dress while Jo carried the pie. Finn pranced through the door and made a beeline for the dog bed next to the fireplace. Luke shook his head and laughed. "He's a goof."

Jo reached for the dress and he held it away from her. "I'll carry it. I can just picture you juggling the pie and sacrificing the dress to save it."

He followed her upstairs and as they walked down the hallway toward her room he stopped outside the door. "You know, I, uh, didn't mean to make you feel uncomfortable when I said you were gorgeous in the dress. I could tell it upset you and that wasn't my intention. I'm sorry."

Jo put her room key against the reader and it clicked open. In addition to her heart beating quicker, it warmed. Not only was he authentic, he was perceptive and not afraid to apologize. She opened the door and motioned him inside.

She put the pie down and took the dress. "I overreacted. Like I said, I don't dress up much and well, uh, I'm just not used to anybody noticing what I look like. So, thank you for the compliment, which is what I should have said earlier."

He let out a long breath and shook his head, smiling. "You're a rarity, Jo."

Her brow creased. "How's that?"

"I've yet to meet a woman as smart and beautiful as you, but yet humble and down to earth. You're special, that's all."

Jo felt that familiar flutter in her chest. "Now you've done it." She grinned and added, "You've called me smart, gorgeous, and beautiful, all in one day. I don't take compliments well, but in my newfound effort to grow as a person, I'll just say thank you, once again."

He took a step toward the door and then turned to her, leaned forward and brushed her lips with his. "The only thing you need to learn to do is to relax. Enjoy your evening, Jo. I'll see you Christmas Day, if not before." He turned the handle and the door shut behind him.

Jo stood rooted to the entryway, both flabbergasted and exhilarated. Her lips tingled and the flutter in her chest had transformed into a pounding hammer. Jo wasn't sure she could wait until Christmas Day.

CHAPTER 7

J o plucked her new clothes from the closet, her heart a bit lighter, as she reflected on what appeared to be genuine love between Alissa and Jed, at least according to what she had witnessed at last night's dinner. When he had faced the women at the table, Jed's eyes had watered with emotion. They all knew his parents were pressuring him and didn't approve of the marriage, but Jo felt his anguish. His mother had never been kind to Alissa, and as Jo listened to him, she sympathized with him, stuck between the two most important women in his life.

With Jo's extensive legal work, she was confident in her ability to see through a fabricated story, and Jed had succeeded in winning her over. He was quite charming and it was easy to see why Alissa loved him so much. His mother, on the other hand, was a vile and despicable human being. The way she had treated Alissa, not to mention her own son, was contemptible. Even Stevie was gracious, or quiet anyway, not voicing any reservations she still might have, seeming to have softened in her opinion of Jed.

Jo shuddered when she thought of becoming part of a

family like his. She hoped Alissa knew what she was getting into and wouldn't regret it later. Jed was lucky to have her by his side, and she hoped their love for each other would get them through what were sure to be rocky times.

Maddie seemed to have enjoyed the evening, and was more relaxed after spending the day coordinating things at the lodge and making sure everything was ready for the ceremony. She had looked tired last night, but happy.

Jo texted Maddie and arranged to stop by her suite for some makeup and accessorizing expertise before the rehearsal dinner tonight. She also wanted to make sure Maddie would be alone, since she hoped to talk to her about Luke.

After she fixed her hair and did her normal makeup routine, which took all of four minutes, she put on the outfit Kathy had helped her find, adding the black open toe sandals. She thought they'd do, but would leave it to Maddie's judgment.

She had time for a quick cup of tea before she headed down the hallway to Maddie's suite. She found Maddie, hair and makeup done, wearing a fluffy robe.

"Oh, I love that outfit. It's perfect," she said, giving Jo a once over after hugging her. "I love that shimmery top with your hair, which looks stunning, by the way."

She brought her fingers to her lips. "Nan's resting in the other room." She took Jo by the hand and guided her into her bedroom area. "Let's take a look through my jewelry. I've got a few things that would look great with that color. Oh, and try my cute black ankle boots with it, that way you'll be warmer than in those sandals."

Jo put on the boots, which fit perfectly, and sat on the bed and watched Maddie paw through her jewelry cases, selecting pieces she thought would work. "So, you've been spending quite a bit of time with Luke?"

Jo blushed and looked up to meet her mother's eyes. "I

bumped into him my first morning here and we just started talking. For the first time in a long time, I'm having fun."

Maddie slipped a bracelet onto Jo's wrist. "You *should* be having fun. You're young and on vacation." She sighed and added, "Do you think it's more than just rekindling an old friendship? Do you have deeper feelings for him?"

Jo admired the bracelet, and tried another one on her other wrist for comparison. "I'm worried I might, but it wasn't in my plan, you know. I don't want to deviate. If I keep going, I can move up to a partner position, build up my investments, all the things I've worked toward and this, whatever this is, it's not part of the future I constructed."

Maddie smiled at her. "Oh, sweetie, there is so much more to life than plans and work. Trust me, if you feel something for Luke, let your heart lead you. Put that big brain of yours in the backseat for once and just follow your heart." She took both of Jo's hands to inspect the bracelets. "I think this one with the multiple thin bangles looks the best."

Jo smiled, thinking of the bracelet she had wrapped for Maddie's Christmas gift. She checked both wrists and agreed that the one with the thin gold strands with a few black ones in between looked best. "What would you think if I told you Luke kissed me?"

Maddie's huge expressive eyes danced with excitement. "Oh, Jo, I would say that is wonderful. He's such a great guy. I remember him from years ago, and always thought he was a neat kid, with a great family, but he's grown into quite an impressive and kind man. Not to mention, handsome, right?"

Jo's cheeks reddened. "I'd have to agree with your assessment." She turned her eyes to the selection of earrings Maddie had unearthed. "I really haven't given him much thought all these years, but I had a little crush on him when I was about twelve. He spent quite a bit of time at the library."

"Smart men are the best and in addition to intelligence,

Luke has such a kind heart. He's wonderful to his parents and Gina. They're just a lovely family." She handed Jo the first pair of earrings and made her turn her head several ways to judge them, then frowned and shook her head, and handed Jo another pair.

Jo used the mirror to insert the wires in her ears. "I've never felt anything like this with any of the guys I've dated, not that I have much experience in that arena. I just feel all tingly and fluttery when I'm around him, even a little impulsive. I find myself thinking about him constantly. It's weird."

Maddie chuckled as she admired Jo in the mirror. "I think those are all signs of attraction, my dear girl."

"But I've got my work to think of. I never planned on romance, at least anything serious, until years down the road."

Maddie shook her head and smiled, taking Jo by the shoulders. "Love doesn't work on a schedule or timeframe. It sometimes comes when you least expect it and is often not convenient. If you're lucky enough to find it, don't let it slip through your fingers. You and I, more than anyone, know how short life can be. Just like I've heard you say to your sisters, you, my sweet, serious, responsible girl, deserve happiness more than anyone I know. Just relax and enjoy all the feels and the joy Luke brings you. Be brave and toss your plans out the window, just until the new year."

Jo touched the dangly gold earrings with the sparkly crystal stones. She turned to her mother and smiled. "I'm not saying anything about Luke to my sisters, not yet. I just don't want to make a big deal about it, you know?"

Maddie nodded and led Jo into the bathroom where Jo sat on a short chair in front of the makeup vanity. Maddie rifled through her case, getting out her eye shadows and pencils. "I understand, believe me. While we're sharing secrets, I've actually been feeling a bit lost lately. I've even thought about selling the house and retiring, moving into something smaller. It's hard to be in that big house all alone."

Jo closed her eyes to let Maddie brush a shimmery gold shadow across her eyelids. As the soft brush glided over her skin, she thought of all the good times she had experienced in that house. It was more than a house; it was a home and a strong symbol of what living there with Maddie and her sisters meant to her. Maddie's love, the family she created, the love of Nan, they were all wound up in memories within the walls of that beautiful house. Flashbacks to birthday parties in the yard, sitting on the porch in the rain, building forts in the backyard with Alissa and Hailey, Stevie cooking them elaborate meals, reading in the leather chair in Simon's study that Maddie had so generously gifted to Jo that first night, filled Jo's thoughts.

Maddie dabbed a tissue under Jo's eyes. "Are you okay?"

Jo nodded. "I love your house. I can't picture you anywhere else."

"I know, it was just a fleeting thought. I'm at a crossroads in my life and experiencing an empty nest, looking at the end of my career and retirement, not to mention perimenopause. Don't get me started on that roller coaster." Maddie reassured her with a smile. "I'm not making any moves and I wouldn't without talking to all of you. I just sense it's time for a change."

She added liner to Jo's eyes and a touch more blush to her cheeks, dabbing a bit of gloss across her lips.

"Speaking of change, it's going to be a different Christmas this year, with Alissa being married," said Jo. "Luke and Gina invited me to Christmas dinner at their house. It feels so strange that we won't all be together like we always have."

"I understand, it's part of what I'm feeling, but we all know the only constant in life is change. You go to Luke's and enjoy yourself. We'll have our Christmas brunch, which I don't expect Alissa and Jed to attend, since it will be their first morning of their honeymoon. We'll just have to be open to new traditions and new possibilities. It's natural that things will evolve, as you girls grow up and get married, have your own families, make your own traditions. Some years I imagine we could have a houseful, with the addition of more sons, like Jed, to our family, and maybe even grandbabies. I have a sense he's going to treasure our family times with his relationship so strained with his parents."

"I felt so sorry for him last night. I can't imagine the stress of it all." Jo took one last look in the mirror, surprised at how a bit of color and pencil here and there really did make a difference. She looked polished and eye-catching, much like her mother. Jo often thought they shared enough characteristics they could have been related by blood. The coppery highlights in Jo's hair matched those in Maddie's, and they shared similar coloring. Jo thought Maddie was beautiful from the first time she saw her and as she got to know her, she realized that beauty wasn't from makeup and clothes. Maddie's beauty came from within and the pretty wrappers she chose only accentuated what was already there.

"What do you think?" asked Maddie, brows raised as she stood behind Jo, gazing at her in the mirror.

"I'm pleasantly surprised. I didn't want to look overly made-up and it's perfect."

"You're beautiful, Jo. More importantly, you're beautiful on the inside. You're strong and smart and so very brave. All I did was dust a little glitter on the outside, but what's inside is what shines through." She kissed her daughter on the top of her head. "I need to get dressed and check on Nan so we can get downstairs."

The rehearsal went smoothly and the food and fun afterward went beyond Jo's expectations. Happy the couple had chosen a casual evening to celebrate the upcoming ceremony, Jo had enjoyed sampling the tasty dishes. Jackson's was the ideal venue and Stevie and the pub's staff had created a menu that fit Jed and Alissa's casual country-loving personalities perfectly.

The best part of the evening had been learning to line dance with her sisters and Maddie. Jed's best man, Mitch, was there and joined in the fun, even sporting a pair of cowboy boots. Jed and Alissa were huge fans of country music and from their skills on the dance floor, were no strangers to line dancing.

The stress of the last few days had been forgotten, as had all the hostility the sisters had felt toward Jed. It was the first chance Jo had to spend an extended amount of time with him and after visiting and watching the two of them together, she realized why Alissa was willing to forgive him and take on his family. When he was next to Alissa, his arm around her, she lit up with happiness. Jo watched them dance a few slow dances together, both of them laughing and whispering in each other's ears as they moved around the dancefloor, entwined together.

It had been a perfect evening and one they all needed. Jo noticed Hailey slip away from the others to visit with Nick, the guitarist connected to Hensley's Sweet Shop. He had kind eyes and longish dark hair favored by most musicians. Jo thought he looked familiar, as in that recognizing him from classes at school way, but not really knowing him. Jo laughed as a musician on the stage treated the crowd to his own rendition of "What the Cowgirls Do", prompting a local woman to lead them in a "Cowgirl Twist" line dance.

Jo took her souvenir cowboy hat, waved goodbye to Hailey who was sitting with Nick, hugged Alissa and Jed, told Stevie how wonderful the food was, and slipped her arm around Maddie's waist as her mom took a sip of water between dances.

Jo wandered back through the lobby, toying with the idea of stopping at the coffee bar to get a hot drink or just making one in her room upstairs. She could already taste the pie she was planning to have while watching a movie. Wondering if they were even open this late, she noticed the lights were still on and ducked her head inside, shocked to find Luke wiping down the counters.

He looked up and smiled, dipped his head in the direction of the hat she was holding. "Howdy, little lady. What can I get you?"

She laughed and said, "I wasn't sure you'd still be open."

"Just getting ready to close, but I can make you something."

"I'd love a chai tea latte, thanks."

He turned to measure the liquids and said, "How was the dinner?"

"It was so fun. I discovered I love line dancing."

"That explains the hat." He finished steaming the milk and added it to the spicy tea mixture. "There you go."

She slid into a chair at the counter. "How come you're working tonight?"

"They needed this shift covered. Someone had a Christmas party to go to and the manager said if I could cover I could have tomorrow off, so that will be three days off in a row with Christmas and the day after. Sounded like a good deal to me." He went about cleaning the machine and closing out the register.

"That's wonderful and it sounds like you deserve some time off." Jo took hold of the cup and started to rise from the chair. "Well, I won't keep you, I'm sure you're tired."

He shook his head. "Not at all. You don't need to run off."

"I was just going to head up to my room and have a piece of that huckleberry pie. Care to join me?"

"I never say no to pie. It's a rule of mine." He grinned and added, "Is it okay if Finn comes with me? He's been camping out behind the front desk."

"Of course. Come on up whenever you're done." Jo slipped the hat on her head, tipped her cup in his direction and added, "See you in a few."

"By the way, you look really nice, Jo."

She smiled, remembering their earlier conversation. She touched her fingers to the edge of her hat. "Why, thank you kindly, sir."

He was still chuckling when she left. Once inside the room, she turned on the television, filled the dog bowl with water, and flicked the switch for the fireplace. She was just considering changing her clothes when she heard three quick knocks on the door.

As soon as she opened it, Finn bounded in, followed by Luke. "That was quick."

"I was just about done when you left, just had to lock up and grab this guy." He pointed to Finn who had already found a cozy spot next to the fireplace.

"Come on in and have a seat. I'll get the pie." She put two pieces on plates and joined Luke on the couch. *Planes, Trains, and Automobiles* was just starting.

Luke pointed at the television. "I love this show. We always watch it at least once during the holidays."

Jo placed the plates on the coffee table. "I'm going to put on some sweats, I'll be right back," she said, hurrying to the bedroom. When she returned, she brought another heavy throw blanket and snuggled into the end of the couch closest to the fireplace, leaving Luke the other end.

In between laughing at the antics of Steve Martin and John Candy, Luke asked about Jo's plans for the rest of her stay at the lodge. "This whole wedding ordeal has taken all my attention and I haven't given much thought to after. I suppose just hang out, take advantage of some of the events they've got going on here for Winterfest, maybe run into town again and catch a movie. Not much really."

"How would you feel about going snowshoeing the day after Christmas?"

Her brows rose as she nibbled on her last bite of pie. "I don't think I've been snowshoeing since I was a kid." She held up her fork. "And don't tell me it's like riding a bicycle. I remember it being harder than it looks."

"It's a fair amount of exercise, for sure. There's a nice trail up by Crystal Lake, with an old cabin up near there. Mr. Jeffries has been having a crew do some remodel work on it. I've taken a few trips up there and saw the trail. It's really peaceful and beautiful."

"I've missed the beauty of the mountains. That sounds like fun."

"Great, we can get you some snowshoes at the ski shop. Just make sure you dress in layers. We can drive part of the way and catch the trailhead and make a loop. I'll pack our supplies and lunch."

"Sounds like a plan. I'll be ready."

Jo glanced over the lodge flyer that she picked up from the end table. "They're having line dancing at Jackson's every night up until New Year's Eve."

"We'll have to get Gina out here one of those nights. She loves to line dance."

"How about you? Do you line dance?"

He feigned shock. "I can't believe you haven't heard of my renowned abilities. I'm famous in some circles."

Jo brewed two mugs of tea while they continued to chat. As the movie ended, another Christmas movie she loved, *The Holiday*, was announced. "Oh, oh, this is one of my favorites. Have you seen it?"

His forehead creased as he watched the preview. "I don't think so. Is it a chick flick?"

She wrinkled her nose. "Well, maybe, sort of, I guess. It's

really good though. But it's got Jude Law and Jack Black, they're manly men, right?"

He grinned and took another cup of tea she offered, pointed at Finn and the soft snores coming from him. "How bad can it be? I'm in."

During commercials and throughout the movie, they talked. The hint of drowsiness Jo had felt when she left the rehearsal dinner was long gone, replaced by the thrill of listening to Luke, and having him show an interest in what she had to say. He talked about how lonely he had felt during his years in the military, despite never really having a minute to himself. He had come to think of his unit as family and told her what a great bunch of guys they were, more like brothers, but he learned the danger in getting too attached to them. Far too many were injured, or lost their lives, and he told Jo how hard it was to get through those dark days.

His experiences and the constant danger had paved the way for his decision to return to Granite Ridge, where he could be close to his family and realign his priorities. He talked about career opportunities he had turned down after leaving the military, telling Jo he was tired of having his days planned by others and wanted to do something he enjoyed, not just make money. He received his MBA while serving, and could have his pick of several positions, but wanted to find the right one.

Listening to him, she understood his desire to help others and make a difference. That was one of many values they shared. That need is what drew her to Love Links. Her job at the law firm met her financial needs, but did little to bring her soul satisfaction.

He loved the outdoors, fishing, hiking, spending time on the water or in the snow; it all appealed to him. He loved dogs and had been a handler for the dog in their unit, Thor, a Belgian Malinois, he had loved. "We retired at the same time," he joked. "I had been thinking about getting out, and took it as a sign when they announced they would be retiring him. I could have stayed four more years and then I'd get a full retirement, but I had a bad feeling. Like I'd used up my good luck, my nine lives, whatever you want to call it. I figured a full retirement wouldn't do me much good if I was dead. I opted to get out, which while not the best financial decision, was the right thing to do. That life takes a toll."

He put his empty mug on the coffee table. "I can make money doing anything, so I decided I'm going to find something I love. In the meantime, I'm enjoying working here, learning to make fancy coffee drinks for uptight city dwellers, and I love walking dogs. They are the best therapists in the business."

Jo smiled. The sadness that had clouded his eyes when he talked about his time in the military evaporated when he mentioned dogs and his family. She saw it was two o'clock in the morning, but couldn't bring herself to suggest ending their night. She reached for his hand and squeezed it. "It takes courage to make a change like you did. I'm glad you decided to come back to Granite Ridge."

He rubbed a thumb over the scar on her hand. "What's this from?"

"Ah, that's a reminder of what I can do when I put my mind to something." She explained that after Grandma Maeve died, she had been placed with a horrible family that lived on a ranch outside of Granite Ridge. "Nobody in the system would listen to me when I tried to tell them they weren't taking care of the foster kids living with them. They used us to perform all the work on the ranch and did nothing to actually care for us."

She took a long sip from her cup. "I spent all my free time in the library at school and had been researching the foster system. I finally figured out how to get the attention of those in charge and made a plan. Not the best plan, but the only thing I could come up with at the time. I rammed a hay hook into my hand knowing they would have to take me to urgent care and a report would get filed."

Luke's brows arched. "I like your spunk and determination, but ouch."

"I know. I probably should have given it more thought. I did clean the hook with rubbing alcohol first, hoping to avoid infection. I also tried to not let it go too deep. It hurt like the devil, but it was worth it. It got me out of there and into Maddie's house. I'm not sure I would have survived if I hadn't done something so drastic."

He ran his fingers over the scar again. "I guess, looking back, it was a small price to pay for what was clearly a defining moment in your life."

Jo's heart warmed as she continued to tell him about her early years and how Maddie was the first person she encountered while in the system that never let her down. Over the years, the system had touted improvements, but Jo knew more could be done and that's why she was so passionate about Love Links and helping kids, especially the older ones, figure out life after foster care. "In some places it's easier to be a foster parent than foster a dog. Not to say that pet parents shouldn't be screened, but jurisdictions are so desperate they approve almost anyone. The system is a mess and I try to concentrate on what I can do and look at the kids I help instead of getting depressed about the bigger picture, but it's hard."

He nodded. "Most big systems are a mess, even it they have good intentions. They get too complicated and lose sight of what's important, their core mission." He took another sip from his cup. "Growing up like that, it wouldn't be easy to trust and like you, I'd want to make sure nothing like that ever happened to me again. I wouldn't want to leave my fate to anyone or any system."

As they talked, Jo felt herself drawn even more to Luke. In addition to having a quick mind and a kind heart, he got her

– really got her. Without explaining it, he understood why she was reluctant to trust, why she focused so much on financial success, and why she missed the warmth of her family more than she could admit. In fact, he might understand her more than she understood herself.

CHAPTER 8

The loud click of the suite door unlocking woke Jo just before ten o'clock on Christmas Eve morning. Blinking her eyes, it took her a few moments to focus. She heard a low bark and a whispered shush, and remembered Finn and Luke.

The last time Jo had looked at the clock, it had been after four in the morning. She had woken with a sore neck from leaning on the arm of the couch, and found Luke sprawled across his end, fast asleep with his head on one of the decorative pillows. With slow movements, she extricated herself from under the throw and covered him with it. She clicked off the television and tiptoed by Finn, who didn't bother opening his eyes, and went to bed.

Jo gasped at the sound of the door closing. She hated Luke to leave without saying goodbye. She threw off the covers and rushed into the living room, where the pillows and blankets lay strewn across the couch, then turned and saw Luke in the kitchen, in his rumpled clothes and bedhead hair, filling the brewing unit with water.

Stevie stood in the entryway, her eyes wide and her mouth gaping. "Sorry," she managed to say, before grinning at Jo and raising her brows even higher. "I guess I should have called first."

Jo felt the heat rise in her cheeks. "No, it's not a problem. We just fell asleep watching movies until early this morning."

"Uh huh." Stevie nodded and turned her back to Luke, giving her sister an exaggerated wink. Jo rolled her eyes and shook her head.

Stevie held up her bag. "I just came to grab a quick soak and to start getting ready for the ceremony. We're supposed to meet in Alissa's room, and Mom and Nan will meet us there to help us get all gussied up." She wrinkled her nose. "I'm not letting them do much in that department."

Jo bobbed her head. "Right, right. You go ahead, bathroom's all yours." Stevie reached down and petted Finn on her way into Jo's bedroom, then whispered cheekily, "I see how it is. One's not enough, huh? You have to keep two handsome guys penned up with you?"

Jo tried – but failed – to smack Stevie as she disappeared into the bathroom.

"I'm so sorry," she whispered to Luke. He just grinned.

"It's not a problem. Trust me. I'm not worried about defending my honor." He returned to his coffee making. "Can I get you a cup?"

She noticed the hint of a smirk on his lips. "You think this is funny, don't you?"

He shrugged. "Maybe a little." He retrieved her cup from the brew station and handed it to her. "Drink this."

A knock on the door interrupted them. "Now, who's here?" Jo stomped over to open it, and found a young bellman with a large pastry box.

She frowned and started to say something when Luke stepped from behind her. "Thanks, Eddie. I owe you one." Before Jo could respond, Eddie disappeared down the hallway.

Jo shook her head and crossed her arms. "So, now

everyone in the lodge is going to think…you know." Luke opened the container and the aroma of fresh pastries filled the air.

"Are those Mabel's?" Jo asked, sniffing and moving toward the box.

"Yes, yes they are." He wiggled his brows at her. "Am I forgiven now?" He pulled out a plate and added a warm almond croissant. "As I remember, this was one of your favorites?"

She swiped the plate from him and took it to the small table. After taking her first bite, she moaned. "Okay, you're forgiven. This may be worth everyone in the lodge thinking I'm a tart."

Luke shook his head laughing. "How old are you? A tart?" He cut another piece of cinnamon roll from his plate. "Trust me, Eddie is the most clueless teenager you will ever meet. He will think nothing of it."

He leaned across the table and kissed Jo, not softly like he did the other night, but with purpose, making her breath catch. "Maybe we should give them all a reason to talk?" His eyes were full of mischief as he pulled away from her.

They heard the sound of the bath water draining and Luke looked at Finn. "I need to take this guy outside and get home." He gestured at the box of pastries from Rusty's Café. "You and your sisters enjoy the rest of those."

He stood, retrieved his jacket, and said, "Last night was the best night I've had in years. Enjoy the wedding and tell your mom hi for me. I'll see you tomorrow night." He grazed his lips against her cheek and made for the door.

Jo was glad she was sitting down. Her legs felt like limp noodles and her whole body tingled. She wondered what would have happened if Stevie hadn't been there.

While bribing Stevie with one of Mabel's huckleberry scones, Jo made her promise not to mention finding Luke in her room. Stevie loved to tease, but in the end agreed to keep it between the two sisters.

Stevie started to take another bite and stopped. "Are you serious about Luke? Are you going to let yourself fall in love with him?"

Her question surprised Jo and she felt the faint lines in the middle of her forehead deepen. "Why would you ask that? It's a little soon for talking of love."

Something about Stevie's body language gave Jo pause, however. Somehow, this wasn't about her and Luke – or at least not just about her and Luke – so she added, "But maybe…I don't know. Why?"

Stevie shrugged as she used to when she first came to live with Maddie and didn't want to answer questions about her past. "I'm just so scared to even consider a serious relationship. What if I'm just like my mother – unable to commit, unable to love, too selfish to have a family of my own? Then there's the whole living in a camper, not really having a steady job thing. Not many people look on a transient lifestyle as favorable."

Jo had never held such disdain for a woman she had never met. Stevie's mom had abandoned her and then manipulated her into forgiving her and going back to live with her more than once. She had a way of getting under Stevie's skin, and like a wasp, always stung her. Jo knew the reason Stevie liked her motorhome, and that hopping from job to job was all about her not wanting to rely on anyone else or give them the power to take away her happiness. Jo had those same feelings with regard to security and her future.

Jo took a deep breath, and then took hold of Stevie's hand. "You are not your biological mother." She reminded Stevie of all the ways she was different and loving, and that despite her sometimes angry outbursts, Jo saw what was inside, in

Stevie's heart: a strong woman who was loyal and a fierce protector of those she loved, traits that were appreciated and cherished.

"Like Maddie says, and shows us every day," Jo added, surprised at the zest in her bolstering speech. "We can choose love and happiness, and we can stitch together a devoted family by always seeing how valuable each of us truly is. We deserve to be loved and to love."

Stevie's eyes brimmed with tears, but a smile filled her face. "You're so wise, Jo. As usual, you've given me a lot to think about. Thank you. I'm so lucky to have you for a sister."

Jo shook her head. "You give me too much credit."

"No," Stevie said, "I don't."

As she looked into her sister's eyes, Jo realized the words she had said to encourage Stevie were the words she needed to hear herself. Maybe, just maybe Luke was the key to her own happiness. But was she brave enough?

In her typical fashion, Stevie was slightly awkward after such an emotional discussion. Then she rallied, and with her characteristic exuberance, promised to make some snacks for Jo and Luke, and even for Finn, and leave them in the refrigerator in the suite so they could enjoy them over the next week. Her gesture warmed Jo's heart and made her want to hug Stevie, despite her sister's discomfort with such displays of affection. Jo settled for smiling at Stevie and placing a hand on her shoulder. "Love you too, sis."

Jo handed Stevie the box of pastries and told her to take them to Alissa's room for fortification while they endured primping. "I'll jump in the shower and be there in a few minutes."

Once Jo finished her shower, she gathered her small makeup bag and traipsed down the hallway in her robe and slippers to Alissa's room. It was a hive of activity, with two hairstylists from the spa swarming over Hailey, having just finished with Alissa's hair.

The chatter and snapping of photos were nonstop in the roomful of women. It took hours, several bottles of champagne, and a Stevie-inspired charcuterie board filled with savory nibbles to get them through the process of hair, makeup, and gown adjustments.

Maddie, who always looked chic, didn't disappoint. She chose a gorgeous dress of pebbled silk in a dusty blue color. The neckline was a thick strand of pearls, crystals, and gorgeous subtle blue and gray stones, bordered by a circle of delicate blue feathers that wrapped around the bodice, brushing over her shoulders. It was a dress made for her and only Maddie could pull off wearing it.

Nan was on hand, dressed in a beautiful gown with a lace bodice and matching lace trimmed jacket in a dusty blue hue that mixed well with the bridesmaids. She looked radiant and her eyes sparkled with delight as she watched her daughter fussing with each of her granddaughter's dresses.

Jo was shocked when the stylists finished with her hair. She never wore her hair up, outside of a pony tail or a quick clip to get it out of the way, but she fell in love with the style that looked like her hair had been woven into a gorgeous loose chignon with tendrils falling around her face. The hairdresser called it a crown braid updo, and as Jo watched her in the mirror, she knew she could never do it herself.

Maddie helped Jo and Stevie with their makeup, since neither of them wore much and weren't as skilled with applying it as the other two women. Then she opened her jewelry cases and let each of the girls choose anything they wanted, guiding them to earrings that would complement the pearl necklaces they were all wearing and would work best with their dresses and hairstyles. For Jo, she helped her choose vintage looking pearl drop earrings with sparkly stones that caught the light.

They toasted with flutes of champagne and as Alissa spoke from her heart and presented each of her sisters with a beautiful charm bracelet, tears brimmed in all their eyes.

Maddie teared up several times as she hugged each one of her girls.

Alissa looked like a princess in her gown with a ballerina bodice and trumpet hem, embellished with hundreds of three-dimensional flowers made from shimmering strands of thread. The entire gown sparkled with thousands of beads and sequins dotting the fabric.

As Maddie helped Alissa with her veil, Jo felt the sting of tears in her eyes once again. She opened them wider, willing herself not to cry and ruin the makeup Maddie had so carefully applied. They took several selfies, with all of them smiling, looking like models in their gorgeous silver and blue gowns and holding mostly white nosegay bouquets. The colors were the perfect palette for a wintery wedding. The luxurious furry wraps around their shoulders only added to the ambience.

The ceremony was held in the gorgeous lobby with the huge fireplace, perfect tree, and stunning view as backdrops. Despite the size of the intimate gathering, the depth of emotion and love emanating from the women who treasured Alissa and welcomed Jed with open arms was palpable. Maddie and Nan sat together and held hands throughout the ceremony, dabbing at their eyes as they watched Jed and Alissa pledge their love to each other.

Jo had been to weddings but had never paid much attention to the vows. Now, the words about trusting each other, being there for each other, and never having to walk alone, hit home. It made her think of Maddie and what she had lost when her husband and young daughter had died. How did she have the strength to survive that depth of sorrow and open her heart to four girls? Jo wasn't sure she could have been that brave.

As soon as the ceremony was over, the photographer posed the group in various spots in the lobby and took hundreds of photos. He moved everyone outside and Maddie made sure he took the shots with Nan first so she could be escorted to the private dining room, where the reception was being held, to wait for the rest of the family.

The snow-covered bridge and walkway made for a gorgeous photo of Alissa and Jed. It was difficult to choose a favorite, but among Jo's was one of all the sisters standing on a blanket of snow, wearing their faux fur wraps, with snow covered mountains and trees in the background.

After almost an hour outside, the wedding party, with rosy cheeks and noses, made their way to the reception. The room was decorated with twinkly lights, branches, and silvery pinecones. Candles flickered on the tables, and flowers that matched the bouquets were everywhere.

As soon as they were seated, drinks were delivered, and Maddie gave the first toast of the night. Mitch stood to give a heartfelt toast to the bride and groom, citing Jed's unwavering love for his new bride. Next, Hailey stood. Jo noticed her hands shaking, and memories of the shy little girl, the first day they met, flashed into Jo's mind. Hailey was much more comfortable with her books and the worlds she created in her writing than being the center of attention.

She spoke about the power of love and family, the idea of being linked together forever, not by blood, but by love. It was a tribute to Alissa and Jed, but the subtext spoke to Maddie and the four girls, and made Jo think of the crooked paths that brought them together and made them soul sisters. Hailey did a fabulous job, and there wasn't a dry eye around the table when she was done.

Once the toasts were applauded, the waiters brought out the first course. Jo sensed such happiness and relief in everyone as they enjoyed the fabulous meal, and witnessed the gentleness between Alissa and Jed.

Finally, the cake was brought in. Alissa teared up when she saw it, rushed to Stevie's side, and hugged her. Stevie had crafted an elegant two-tiered cake in the most subtle of blue, like a whisper of the dusty color Alissa favored. In addition to the wide lace ribbon circling each tier, she'd placed white camellias, silver leaves, and tiny pinecones with dusty blue berries to accent it perfectly. The cake looked too pretty to eat, but after several photos, Jed and Alissa held the knife, and cut the first slice. The cake turned out to be as scrumptious as it was stunning, with the layers of raspberry and cream filling melting in Jo's mouth.

The photographer interrupted the dessert to lead Jed and Alyssa outside, hurrying them so as not to miss what he termed the perfect window of opportunity. Jo couldn't resist and followed them outside to the rear of the lodge, where the photographer had them stand on the top step, with the dark sky filled with millions of stars behind them. Alissa's dress and the snow below sparkled with the soft glow from the lights along the steps. The new bride and groom kissed, and the photographer captured what Jo knew was the magical shot Alissa had wanted.

Shivering, despite her wrap, Jo hurried through the door and into the main lobby. She stopped by the fireplace to warm herself and when she turned to go back to the dining room, she ran into Luke and Gina, leaving the restaurant.

Gina, dressed in a festive deep green velvet dress, reached for Jo's hands. "You look stunning. I bet the wedding was beautiful."

Jo smiled. "It was perfect." She pointed to the door. "I just ran outside to watch them take one more picture. I've forgotten how incredible the night skies are here, with all the stars. It made for an unforgettable photo."

"That sound so romantic." Gina poked her brother with her elbow. "Doesn't it, Luke?"

He grinned and nodded with his eyes fixated on Jo. "Yes, I'm sure it was." He cleared his throat. "You do look spectacular."

Jo regarded Luke, wearing dark jeans and a dark blue jacket over an iridescent dress shirt that was somewhere between eggplant and indigo. Her heart beat a little faster as she admired him. "Thank you. You're looking very handsome tonight as well, and I love your dress, Gina."

Gina glanced at her tongue-tied brother and said, "I'm so excited you're coming tomorrow. It will be fun to have company. It's a bit lonely without Mom and Dad here…and my girls." Gina's eyes filled with tears.

"Is there anything I can bring?" Jo added, "Or, maybe I should say have Stevie make and bring? I'm not known for my cooking skills."

Gina's smile returned. "I've got everything we need. Just bring yourself." She glanced at Luke. "We should probably get home and make sure the dogs haven't destroyed the place." Gina hugged Jo, and turned to Luke. "I'm going to collect our coats. I'll meet you at the door."

As Gina walked away, Luke took both of Jo's hands in his, and met her eyes. "Your hands are still cold." He rubbed his thumbs over them, and leaned closer to whisper in her ear, "I'm glad I got the chance to see you." He let his lips linger on the side of her neck.

Chills rippled through her. "Me too," she murmured, wishing they were alone instead of in a lobby full of people.

"Merry Christmas, Jo," he said, pulling away from her. "See you tomorrow."

Jo waved goodbye to them, and made her way back to the dining room, arriving right before the photographer. Jed and Alissa returned a few minutes later. They thanked everyone for the wonderful wedding and all they had done to make it happen, then moved to the dance floor and their first dance as husband and wife.

Jo spent the rest of the evening thinking of Luke, as she danced with Jed and Mitch, visited with Nan, and sat with her mom, basking in the glow of happiness. Alissa had asked the wait staff to box up slices of cake for everyone to take back to their rooms, and Jo snagged her share on her way upstairs.

When she got to her room, she took one last look in the mirror, knowing she wouldn't be dressing up like this again until another one of her sisters decided to marry. She smiled when she saw a new pair of red flannel pajamas, wrapped with a sparkling ribbon, atop her pillow. Mom, just like that first Christmas, never failed to make sure they all got new pajamas. She texted Maddie to tell her she loved them and loved her.

After she changed into the pajamas, she brewed a mug of tea and snuggled into the couch to watch *It's a Wonderful Life*. She missed having Luke and Finn there. She'd always loved watching movies in her apartment, but after having had such an enjoyable evening with Luke, she wasn't sure if watching a movie alone would ever be the same.

She longed for the weight of him against her, the warmth of his shoulder next to hers, the feel of his fingers rubbing her hand. She sniffed at the throw blanket and shut her eyes, absorbed in the spicy scent that still lingered, reminding her of another thing she missed.

CHAPTER 9

Christmas morning, Jo took her time getting ready, lounging in bed watching one of her favorite Christmas movies, *The Christmas Card.* This would be the first Christmas without all their traditions. Maddie had told each of them last night that Alissa was going to skip the morning gift exchange and brunch this year, since it would be her first morning as a new bride. She and Jed were ensconced in the honeymoon cabin, and Maddie had assured them they should just enjoy their time together.

Jo would have preferred they were all together back at the house in Granite Ridge. She loved Christmas at Maddie's house. The huge tree was always piled with gifts, and Stevie and Maddie worked in the kitchen to make a magnificent breakfast, always including blueberry waffles in memory of Simon. Watching everyone open their gifts was the highlight, and this year it just wouldn't be the same.

Like Maddie had said, it was inevitable that things would change and each of them would be making their own traditions. Instead of concentrating on what felt like the loss of Alissa and their Christmas morning routine, Jo thought ahead to spending the evening with Luke. She dressed in her favorite jeans, a black shirt, and her new burgundy poncho. She added Maddie's black boots, fixed her hair, and collected her wrapped gifts before heading to Maddie's suite, where her mother had arranged a catered brunch.

Stevie whooped and cheered when she opened the box with her colorful new clogs. She put them on and traipsed around the suite, then hugged Jo and kissed her all over her face. Hailey ran her fingers over the soft leather journal engraved with her name, before rewarding Jo with a long hug, and telling her she would treasure it always. Nan loved the cashmere shawl and put it on, telling Jo it was perfect for the chilly winter days.

But nothing had prepared Jo for Maddie's reaction to the bracelet. She stared at it, her mouth gaping, tears rolling down her cheeks. She put it on her wrist and swore she would never take it off, kissing Jo and showing the other girls how beautiful it looked. "I just love how all the individual bracelets are held together with the little heart charm, since that is exactly what holds all of us together."

While Maddie repaired the damage to her makeup, she added a bit of color to Jo's eyelids and lips, slipping a lip gloss in her hand. "Take this, it looks great with your sweater."

The women sat around the beautiful table in the presidential suite, with the stunning view of the snow-covered mountains. The food was delicious, but nothing compared to what Stevie and Maddie always made.

Whatever happened in the future, Jo hoped nobody else would get married at Christmas, so they could spend the holiday together at Maddie's. As she pondered past Christmases, she realized it might be easier to have their first Christmas morning without Alissa here at the lodge, rather than at the house where her absence would be amplified. This may have been Maddie's way of easing them into making new memories and introducing them to the idea of new traditions.

The conversation shifted from reliving moments from the wedding to plans for the rest of the day. Hailey was the first to chime in, and told the others Nick had invited her to join him for Christmas dinner. Stevie planned to spend the day in her motorhome, relaxing after all the wedding excitement. After their revelations, Jo didn't feel so awkward, and divulged she was having dinner with Luke and Gina.

With concern in her eyes, Hailey turned to Maddie. "That leaves you and Nan all alone. I wouldn't have said yes to Nick if I would have known everyone was going to be gone."

Maddie waved her hand in the air. "That's fine. Nan and I have an ongoing card game we plan to finish, and there's enough food leftover that we won't need to leave this room for days. Please, don't worry about us. I want you all to enjoy your holiday and your time at the lodge however you choose."

Jo wished Maddie had someone special in her life, someone with whom she could spend Christmas. She, more than anyone, deserved a second chance at love. But maybe too much change all at once would be overwhelming.

Maddie's phone chimed, and she shared a link the photographer had sent her. He had a site where all the untouched photos could be viewed. The women stared at their phones as they scrolled through the photos, from them getting ready to Jed and Mitch helping each other with their ties. They oohed and aahed at the group in the snow, and Maddie teared up when she saw the one with the starry sky.

Jo gasped when she flicked to a few of her and Luke in the lobby. The photographer had captured him gazing at her, a look of pure adoration in his eyes. The next photo showed him whispering in her ear and a smile on her face. He even caught one of them standing close to each other, right before Luke kissed her. From her chair, Stevie raised an eyebrow.

"My, my, it's always the quiet ones," she teased. "You saw Luke *again* last night?"

Jo shrugged. "I ran into him and Gina when I was coming back inside last night. They had Christmas Eve dinner here."

"And…" prodded Stevie.

"And, nothing. We chatted for a few minutes and they left. I didn't know the paparazzi was watching."

"Luke's a great guy, always so friendly and helpful to everyone in town," said Hailey. "I didn't know you were seeing him."

Jo shook her head. "I'm not sure I'm seeing him. We just reconnected. I used to visit with him at the library. Truth be told, I had a little crush on him." Jo used her thumb and index finger to indicate a tiny space.

Stevie grinned. "Well, he's all grown up now, and I'd say he's the one with the crush." She narrowed her eyes. "Seriously, Jo, it's like we talked about. You're entitled to be happy. All you do is work and volunteer. You never take time off to relax, so have a little fun. And, I agree, you couldn't find a nicer guy than Luke."

Maddie raised her champagne glass and tilted her head at Jo. "Trust your heart. It won't lead you astray."

"I do find myself attracted to him," Jo confessed. "But it's not very practical, since I'm flying back to Chicago in a week."

Maddie rose from her chair and came behind Jo, resting her hands on Jo's shoulders. "Don't look too far ahead. Enjoy today, every single moment. Otherwise, happiness will pass you by while you're worrying about tomorrow. Things that are meant to be have a way of working themselves out, trust me." She kissed the top of Jo's head.

Maddie's kitchen counter held all the flower arrangements from the reception, and she urged each of them to take an arrangement or two. Jo thought one of them would make a lovely hostess gift for Gina.

After brunch, Jo stopped by the gift shop and picked up two bottles of wine and a selection of craft brews for Luke, and put them in the Jeep. She took a few minutes to check her appearance, something she never even thought of before this past week, then grabbed her purse and a centerpiece from the reception, and headed down the mountain.

Jo checked house numbers as she drove down Pine Street, then recognized Luke's truck and pulled to the curb. The four dogs made for an excited welcoming party on the porch. Luke, wearing a flour covered apron, rescued her and relieved her of the bottles of beer and wine. When he led her into the house, an enticing aroma greeted her.

She thought she detected turkey, but then smelled something that reminded her of pizza. She followed her confused nose through the living room and dining room, then into the kitchen, where Gina was busy at the cooktop stirring a pot, the source of the heavenly smell. The kitchen was mostly white and full of light, with a huge cooktop and two wall ovens. Baking sheets, flour, and bowls covered the granite counter.

"You're just in time to help with our traditional ravioli making," said Luke, putting the beer in the fridge. He poured Jo a glass of wine, and added a bit more to his and Gina's glasses to finish off the bottle they had started. "First rule of ravioli making, you have to drink wine while doing it."

Gina wiped her hands on her apron and joined them at the island counter. "Our mom, Maria, is half Italian and always makes ravioli. Dad is mostly Irish, so we blend the two together for the meal." She blew her bangs off her forehead. "Bottom line, we are going to have way too much food, but we won't have to cook for a week."

Luke pointed at the pasta machine, and explained Gina would run the dough through it until it was the perfect thinness for ravioli. "Mom always says if you hold it up and can see the shadow of your hand behind it, you know it's right."

Gina began sliding a piece of dough through it.

"Once she gets that done, we'll work on adding fillings and then cut them out." He pointed at the mixtures in the bowls. "We have sausage, mushroom, and a pumpkin pinenut mix."

While Gina continued to run pieces of dough through the machine, Luke hurried to the cooktop to stir the pots. "We've got Mom's roasted garlic sauce and brown butter sauce cooking."

Jo's eyes widened as she took in the operation. "You guys must have been cooking all morning."

Gina nodded. "It's tons of work, but really fun. It just wouldn't be Christmas without all this."

The kitchen was plenty warm, prompting Jo to slip off her poncho, and Luke gave her a "Kiss me, I'm Irish" vivid green apron to wear. Over the next couple of hours, Jo helped Luke spoon fillings onto the dough, became an expert at egg washes, and had fun using the cutters to create the square and round pillows of dough.

While she and Luke made what must have been hundreds of ravioli, Gina took care of making the sides to go with the turkey and ham in the oven. Luke took several baking sheets filled with ravioli into the garage and put them in the freezer, then went about filling a pot with water to boil those that remained. Jo was surprised to learn they needed to boil for less than five minutes.

With the prep work done, he and Jo tackled the dishes. After hanging up their damp towels, he grabbed a cold beer and offered Jo more wine.

She held up her hand. "I think I could use some water."

He fixed a glass, adding a slice of lemon, and motioned her to follow him. "I'll give you a quick tour of the place while we wait for dinner." He led the way out of the kitchen and into a short hallway that opened into a study or den, outfitted with a television and comfortable furniture. He gestured at the space. "So, I took over this section when I moved back. Turned the study into my personal mini-living room, so I can watch whatever I want. A houseful of girls takes me back to my younger days, and Gina knew I'd need some drama-free space of my own."

"It looks great," Jo said, and followed him past his living room, into his large bedroom and ensuite master bathroom.

"I tackled sprucing this up a bit. Put in new flooring, painted, had a friend help me do the bathroom."

Jo noticed a huge walk-in shower, using the same over-sized tiles on the floor, but accented with gorgeous glass tiles in browns and copper tones.

Luke pointed at the walk-in closet, most of it empty except for one section that held his clothes. "That's it for my domain. Gina has the other downstairs bedroom at the front of the house, sort of a mirror of this one, just without the extra room."

He guided Jo back to the main part of the house, stopping at the living room and dining area. "Gina and the girls use this living room, and the girls' bedrooms and bathroom are upstairs. Then there's a powder room and a laundry room off the kitchen, and a nice porch in the back, which is where the four dogs are for the moment. They have a mountain of new toys to play with and they can get underfoot in the kitchen."

"I love porches. Another thing you don't get with an apartment. This is a lovely home and so roomy for everyone. I like these old houses," said Jo, admiring the crown molding.

"It needs a little updating, but Gina is tackling it a little at a time. The kitchen was her first priority, and she had that done before I came home. Like Mom, she's a great cook."

"I can see that. She and Stevie share that passion. I love to eat, but don't cook much."

"Then you're in for a real treat. You won't go away hungry

here, and Gina is so happy to have you. She really misses her girls and we both miss Mom and Dad."

The emotion in his voice reached all the way to his eyes, and she reached for his hand. "I was feeling a little blue myself, with this being the first Christmas we haven't all spent at Maddie's house. With Alissa getting married, it changes our traditions. So, I'm grateful to be here with you and Gina."

He inched closer to her and met her lips with his, deepening the kiss as a quiet moan escaped from her. Jo's toes curled inside her boots. She couldn't get enough of the scent of him, the feel of his soft lips against hers. When he freed her lips, he grinned, tilted his forehead to meet hers. "I'm all for new traditions, as long as they include you."

Jo was stuffed after sampling all the delicious flavors of ravioli she had helped make, smothered in homemade sauces, along with the traditional fare she was used to eating for Christmas dinner. To top it off, Luke had ordered two pies from Mabel, a gorgeous chocolate cream covered in chocolate curls and a special lemon meringue she made known as Luke's lemon pie, which was extra tart with a mile-high meringue.

Jo helped Luke take the dogs for a walk after dinner, covering the blocks near Gina's house, including the block where Maddie lived. Jo walked Otis and Watson, since they went everywhere together, and Luke took charge of Finn, who liked to hold his leash in his mouth, and Tumbleweed, who wasn't as well trained as the others. Luke set a slow pace, allowing them to appreciate the festive neighborhood.

It was cold, but a perfect, clear evening with plenty of illumination from the streetlights and Christmas lights decorating the neighborhood. The indigo sky, scattered with millions of twinkling stars above, and the festive lights in the trees and bushes, made for an unforgettable sight. Luke reached for Jo's hand, and held it as they wound their way through the dazzling streets.

When they returned home, the dogs snuggled together in the living room. Jo and Luke helped Gina finish tidying the kitchen, and then the three of them played board games. Jo laughed until her stomach ached when they played a game of wits requiring players to shout out answers before their opponents.

Jo's love of movies worked in her favor as many of the categories had to do with movies or television shows. While they played, Luke talked about their snowshoeing outing, and they agreed to take off at first light, after having an early breakfast at the lodge. That way, they would have time to get to the cabin, have lunch, and get back by mid-afternoon. "Finn's going to stay with Gina at the store, since there are some snowmobile trails nearby and I'd rather play it safe."

Gina hurried to the entry closet. "That reminds me, I have some good snow boots for you, Jo. Tons of sizes, so feel free to go through them and take anything that works."

Jo thanked her, and found a pair that were much more suitable and weather-ready than the boots she had brought with her. She left them by the front door so she wouldn't forget them when she left.

They played a word game that challenged each player to identify the bogus definition of obscure words. The more wine Gina drank, the funnier her responses became. Again, Jo won, and credited her experience with weird legal words and Latin terms as giving her an edge.

As much as Jo hated to leave, after sampling the delicious pies and another mug of tea, she collected her coat and the borrowed boots. Gina embraced her in a long hug, and wished her a Merry Christmas before making herself scarce in the kitchen. Luke linked his fingers in Jo's as he walked her out to the porch and down the sidewalk, lingering as he kissed her. The feel of his strong fingers on the back of her neck and his soft lips against hers made her forget how cold it was outside. When they finally broke apart, he took hold of her hands and she looked up at the blanket of twinkling stars in the night sky. It had been a magical night and she didn't want it to end. She'd be happy to stay like this, wrapped in his arms, under the glittering stars forever.

"I hate to think of you all alone in your hotel room."

She giggled, a bit nervous as she fantasized about him coming back with her. "I'll be fine. I'll meet you downstairs at six-thirty."

She started to get into the driver's seat, but then made the mistake of looking back at Luke, and the next thing she knew, she stood in front of him again, and he was kissing her. She put her arms around his neck and clung to him, her heart hammered in her chest, as warmth flooded through her body. She didn't want to leave; didn't want to let go. Being here, with him, was a feeling like no other. Every nerve in her body was on high alert and his touch sent shivers through her. Despite telling herself this attraction she felt was because of the holiday and nostalgia, she couldn't stop measuring time by when she would see him again. Just over six hours now, but as she tasted the lemon on his lips and felt his fingers in her hair, those few hours felt like an eternity.

CHAPTER 10

I t was still dark when Jo dressed in as many layers as she could muster and noticed a text from last night she had missed from Stevie. It showed her cuddling a cute puppy she named Syd. He was an unexpected Christmas gift. She didn't divulge much more than that, but seeing the genuine happiness in her smile as she held the little bundle of fur warmed Jo's heart. She tapped a few heart and dog emojis before leaving her room.

She met Luke in the Cedar Mountain Restaurant at the crack of dawn, which hadn't actually cracked yet, where he already had a table in front of the blazing fire. He stood when she arrived, and greeted her with a kiss on the cheek. As she was perusing the menu, her phone chimed with a voicemail.

She saw it was Doris, and asked Luke if he would mind her listening to it. As she held the phone to her ear, her smile faded and her forehead creased with worry. She disconnected, and shook her head. "My neighbor, Doris, she's in her seventies and went to Texas to stay with her son for the holidays. She fell and had to have surgery on her hip, and has made the decision to move to stay with them." Jo's eyes glinted with tears.

Luke reached across the table for her hand. "I'm sorry. I take it you were close?"

Jo nodded. "Honestly, she's my closest friend in Chicago. I don't know what I'll do without her there." Jo shook her head.

Their waitress came over, offered drinks, and took their order. Luke checked his phone and nodded. "I've been keeping an eye on the weather and it still looks good. A storm is supposed to come in late tonight but we'll be home in time for dinner."

The waitress delivered Jo's tea and freshened his coffee. Jo swallowed several sips, laced with honey, and focused on Luke instead of how lonely she would be without her neighbor and friend.

"Speaking of dinner, Gina says to come over. You've got to help us eat our way through the leftovers." Luke met her eyes.

"You don't have to twist my arm. It was all delicious. I've never had homemade ravioli."

Luke added some huckleberry jam to his toast. "The girls won't be home until New Year's Day, so I asked Gina about line dancing and she's in. You pick the night that's best for you, and we can do dinner, make an evening of it."

"Any night this coming week will work. There was some talk of going to karaoke, but I'm not sure which night." She knew her face was expressing her dislike, but still didn't expect Luke's response.

He gasped. "You're kidding, right? Oh, we have to go. It's so fun."

"I have a terrible singing voice," she said, rolling her eyes.

"Everybody does. That's what makes it great." He signed the check and pulled Jo's chair out for her, helping her with her coat. It had been ages since Jo had been in the company of a true gentleman.

As they went through the front door, Jo said, "I was

thinking we should take my Jeep. That way we could keep all our gear inside, plus it's capable in the snow."

He nodded as he led the way to the parking lot. "I'll just grab my stuff and the backpacks. I already reserved your snowshoes at the ski rental desk."

After a quick detour to pick up Jo's equipment, Luke drove them to the parking lot where they could join the trailhead. She tried to help unload the gear but couldn't even budge his huge backpack. He helped her secure the small backpack he had filled with food and snacks. Then, he showed her how to get in and out of her snowshoes, and handed her the poles. "Remember, if you can walk, you can snowshoe."

She shook her head at his less than helpful wisdom, as she watched him swing the heavy pack onto his shoulders. "What do you have in there to make it so heavy?" she asked.

"Ah, this isn't heavy. You should have seen the gear I carried for work. I've just got backcountry essentials in here. What I always take with me when I'm hiking."

They set off, with him leading the way. The scenery was majestic, with tall trees along the path, dripping with snow. The crust glittered under the first hints of sunlight, and the air smelled fresh. It was peaceful and quiet, except for a few rabbits and squirrels that scampered along the trail.

Luke stopped at a turn and held up his hand in a fist. Jo looked where he pointed. A herd of deer! Jo scrambled to get her phone out of her pocket, as the deer walk into the trees, disappearing from view right as she was ready to take a photo.

Luke trekked forward and Jo followed until they stopped by an icy stream, frozen except for a thin trickle of water. They rested on a rock and watched a few rabbits and squirrels dart amongst the trees. He retrieved two bottles of water from his pack and gave her one.

Jo took the opportunity to capture some photos of the

gorgeous forest and mountain views. "This is so beautiful. I'm glad you thought of coming up here."

"I'm so glad you like it too." He tucked the empty bottles into her backpack, and they set out again.

Despite the dark clouds beginning to move over the mountains and the increasing coolness of the morning air, Jo worked up a bit of a sweat and removed her scarf, stuffing it inside her jacket. It took them almost three hours to get to the cabin. During the last twenty minutes of their trek, soft snowflakes began to fall. They left their snowshoes on the covered porch, next to a stack of firewood, and Luke used a key to open the front door. He looked up at the mountain range above them, and shook his head. "Storm's moving in early."

"Oh, no. Shall we turn back?" Jo eyed the ominous looking clouds.

He shook his head. "We'll be safer here where we can take advantage of having dry shelter."

He motioned her inside, and said, "This was dilapidated, but Mr. Jeffries wanted to get it in shape and offer it as a rustic retreat, especially for fishermen and backcountry hikers, or people who just want to get away from it all."

Jo stepped through the door and was greeted by the smell of fresh cut wood and sawdust. The exterior had been completed with a new metal roof, new windows, and siding. The interior was in progress but clean and smelled of fresh paint.

Luke grimaced and said, "Rustic is a code word for no bathroom due to not wanting to mess with a septic system, so if you need the use of one, there is a brand-new outhouse out back. We do have a generator system for power and running water."

"I'm good, thanks," said Jo, looking around the cabin. The furnishings were sparse, with all the new furniture still in boxes to keep it clean, while they finished the interior work.

Luke unpacked containers from their backpacks, lining up ham and turkey sandwiches, fruit, potato chips, and pieces of pie on the bare wooden counter. He even had a thermos of hot chocolate.

They sat on a wooden bench and took in the view from the French doors at the back of the cabin as they ate. As the trees swayed in the wind and the clouds that loomed over the mountains darkened the sky, Jo tried to keep her nerves in check.

Even though it was warmer inside the cabin, it was still getting colder. Jo was thankful for the hot chocolate, and drank two mugs full while she ate the scrumptious leftovers. As they ate, Luke's phone beeped with a weather alert. He read the screen.

"This isn't good. They've just updated the forecast and issued a new warning. They expect blizzard like conditions and higher amounts of snow in the next few hours."

He flicked through more screens and turned to Jo. "I don't want to chance making it back to the Jeep with this fast-moving system, we could get stuck out on the trail in a blizzard. It's probably safer to stay here until it passes."

"You mean stay the night here?" Jo felt her mouth go dry.

"And digging out in the morning. It's supposed to be better by then." He glanced out the window again. "But we'll have a fair amount of new snow to traverse."

Jo studied the threatening dark clouds. The beautiful sunshine from the morning had evaporated. "I definitely don't want to get stuck on the trail. Will we be safe here?"

"Sure, we'll be fine. I'll call Gina and let her know, so nobody will worry about us. We've got a limited amount of fuel for the generator, which means no power. I brought a battery pack, but it probably won't do us much good. Cell service will most likely go out during the storm." Luke began to take inventory of firewood and other essentials, went outside and started the generator to run the pump, while Jo scouted out the pallets of supplies and furnishings, looking for kitchen pots and pans.

She located several boxes on one pallet and then texted her mom to let her know where she was and that they planned to take the trail back to the Jeep in the morning as soon as the weather permitted.

Luke returned and cut the straps on the pallet she had discovered. Together, they unearthed the kitchen supplies from the boxes and went about filling pots and pans with water. Luke surveyed the interior and said, "Go ahead and start gathering up all the wood scraps scattered about the cabin. That will work for kindling, and we can get a fire started."

Jo went about her task, using an empty box to carry all the scraps of wood piled in each of the rooms. When she arrived back in the living area, Luke was unpacking the backpacks, lining up the contents on a new interior door he had placed atop two sawhorses. Jo gawked at the array of items – flashlights, batteries, a lighter and matches, GPS unit, headlamp, space blankets, first aid kit, folding shovel, ice axe, extra socks, hand and foot warmers, binoculars, hand sanitizer, a small container of duct tape, zip ties, tools, and a portable water filter, not to mention food, bottled water, snacks, and a big orange sleeping bag.

"Wow," she said, fixating on the collection of survival gear. "When you said a few essentials, you meant it."

He stacked the extra sandwiches in the large windowsill in the kitchen. "They'll be cold enough there." He turned to Jo. "We're lucky we have the cabin for shelter. We won't need most of this stuff, but if we were stuck out there," he pointed out the window, "we'd need it all."

Jo placed some cardboard and the scrap wood she'd gathered into the fireplace, as Luke carried firewood inside from the front porch.

The wind was picking up and blew frigid air through the

open door. "If you need to use the outhouse, probably best to get out there now before it gets any worse." Luke gestured with his head to the side of the cabin, his arms full of firewood.

"Okay, be right back." Jo found the facilities clean and not even close to as horrible as she had imagined. As she walked back to the cabin, the wind gusted against her, making her lean into it to make any headway. Glad they weren't trying to get back to the Jeep in this weather, and even more grateful for the cabin, she stomped the snow from her boots and opened the door. A blazing fire roared in the stone fireplace.

"It's getting nasty out there," she said, moving to warm her hands.

"There's a couch in one of those big boxes in that back room. I was thinking we could unpack it and use it tonight. Set it up here in front of the fireplace. Better than lying on the hard floor all night, don't you think?"

Jo bobbed her head in agreement. In the back room, Luke flipped open the menacing looking blade on the multi-tool he pulled from his pocket, and popped out the staples. "I'm hoping we can do this without ripping up the box so we can shove the couch back in tomorrow before we leave, to keep it from getting dirty."

The wind howled and snow pelted against the windows as they worked to preserve the packing materials and box. The dark brown leather couch was heavy, and Jo wasn't much help maneuvering it to the living area, doing more guiding than lifting. Luke heaved it into place and unzipped his sleeping bag. He added a small box as a makeshift end table and put a flashlight, lighter, and a few other supplies on it. Finally, he surveyed the space. "Okay, I think we're about as set as we can be. Water, shelter, food, and a fire. That's more than enough to get us by until morning."

Jo peeked out the backdoor, watching the tops of the huge pine trees bend in the wind screaming off the mountain. This was one of the few times in recent memory that she could recall relying on someone other than herself. It wasn't lost on her that if Luke hadn't been with her, she would have struggled, not knowing what to do and not having his expertise. Maybe all that wedding talk about two being stronger together was true.

Jo hadn't brought her phone charger, but Luke charged his phone before turning off the generator. He flicked through his screens and nodded. "Gina said she'll let Mr. Jeffries know we're taking shelter up here, and asked me to text her first thing tomorrow. If she doesn't hear from us in the morning, she'll send help."

He grabbed the hand and foot warmers and told Jo she could put them in her boots and pockets tonight, and explained they last up to twelve hours. "I've got enough to get us through tonight and we can use them on our way out tomorrow."

"I'll be fine with the fire. I don't want to waste them."

The windows rattled as the wind speed increased, and just before three o'clock in the afternoon, they lost cell service.

Darkness settled in early around the cabin, and the two of them huddled together, watching the flames lick the logs as they savored the warmth of the fire and each other. Between more than a few playful kisses and catnaps, and long periods of thinking on Jo's part, they played Twenty Questions and Two Truths and a Lie. They laughed at the zany lies they each came up with, and Jo learned that she and Luke shared a fear of clowns and that he could play the piano.

They ate a late dinner of sandwiches and pie, then boiled some water to make soup from the packets Luke had in his backpack, instead of drinking the hot chocolate. That they would save for breakfast.

The howling winds kept at it into the night, but Luke kept the fire fed and under the cover of his sleeping bag, they were warm and cozy.

Jo wasn't sure why, but talking in the darkness was easier than in a well-lit room. She divulged how incredibly lonely she was in Chicago, and how much she dreaded going back there. Other than the time she spent at Love Links and connections she made with some of the foster children, Doris had been the one bright spot and constant in her rather solitary personal life. Without her, the apartment wouldn't be the same.

"There's nothing special about the law firm, but they treat me well and I feel a certain loyalty to them, having worked there since college. My work at Love Links is really the only time I feel that deep satisfaction that comes from doing transformational work. Being here, being home with everyone, being with you..." She paused to touch her hand to the side of Luke's face. "It has made me realize just how empty and unhappy my life is."

He kissed her palm and said, "You know you have the power to change things if you aren't happy, right?"

"Hmmm, a change just isn't in my plan." This whole trip, being here with her mom and sisters, and with Luke, it was just an escape from reality, more like a fantasy. She had her real life back in Chicago, back at her desk where she'd soon make partner and beef up her investment accounts. All this, these weird and wonderful flutters and feelings weren't real. It was foolish to think they were anything beyond reliving a bit of her youth with the first boy who had been her friend and was now all she imagined and more.

"I think happiness trumps plans. In fact, I'm walking proof of just that. I know what you mean about a plan. I had planned to stay four more years and get my twenty, but I finally realized it wasn't worth it and I'm so much happier now."

She pondered his words. "I have a financial goal and need to keep working to reach that, so I never have to worry about the future or have to depend on anyone else."

He ran his finger along her cheek. "I understand. The business side of me admires your resolve, but the other side of me thinks you deserve more."

Neither of them said anything for several minutes, staring instead at the flickering orange and gold flames. Luke turned to her and snuggled her closer to him. "Okay, I'm going to ask you some questions and you can't think, you just have to answer truthfully, the first thing that pops into your mind. Agreed?"

She nodded, resting her head against his shoulder.

"What gives you joy?"

"I don't know."

"Okay, we'll go back to that one. When do you feel the most passionate?"

Jo almost said, "Being with you," but controlled herself just in time. "Um, my work?"

"If it's a question, then that's not it. When do you feel the most passionate?"

Love Links, maybe, thought Jo. No. Not the organization. It was deeper than that. "Making a difference in the lives of those kids."

"What are you most grateful for?"

"Not what, who. Maddie, and my sisters too, for being my family."

"What would you do if you didn't have to make money anymore?"

Again, Jo didn't know what to say.

"There are no wrong answers. In this second, what would you do if you didn't have to make money anymore?"

Jo laughed. "You're persistent, aren't you?"

Luke's eyes smiled down on her. "You have no idea. So, what would you do?"

Jo grew serious under his gaze. "I'd do more than fight for the kids in court. I'd… I don't know. It's silly."

"No," Luke whispered. "It's not."

"I… I'd do everything I could to make sure they had family; people they knew cared about them." She bit her lip, then continued. "And I'd do it here, in Granite Ridge."

"What's your biggest regret?"

That one stopped her cold. As she contemplated, she swallowed hard. "Missing out on my family and being so far away. Being alone."

A sense of peace engulfed her, simultaneously lifting a heavy weight from her shoulders. Luke squeezed her hand and said, "Okay, so now you have a vision for the future you'd like to create. All you have to do is outline the steps to get you there."

They talked until the wee hours of the morning, with Luke sharing that he had been working on a new vision of his own. He wanted to start an outdoor business where he'd serve as a fishing guide, hiking guide, maybe offer some survival skills, and even summer camps. Mr. Jeffries had proposed that the lodge could feature and recommend Luke's business and send him clients, and even offered his staff to help coordinate bookings.

"That sounds like the perfect business for you," said Jo. "You'd be doing what you love."

Luke nodded. "The old saying of 'doing what you love means you'll never work a day in your life' was what I thought about when I came up with the idea. The investment would be relatively small, so if it doesn't work, it wouldn't be much of a risk."

Jo steered the conversation to ideas for Luke's new venture, but he stopped her short when he asked, "So, what's your first step in making your wish a reality? You light up, even with how dark it is in here, when you talk about your family and helping foster kids. I can see the happiness in your face, even feel it, when you mention your passion. I know you could make it work."

She chuckled at his seriousness. It was just a game, but she played along. "Figuring out my financial plan, if I take this little detour, would be my first priority."

Luke's grin was visible in the light of the fire. "Tomorrow, we'll work on that and I can help you with a business plan."

She loved his enthusiasm and the sparkle in his eyes with the flames reflected in them. It just seemed like folly. How could she give up her stable career and risk all her plans?

He hugged her closer. "You know I'm falling in love with you, right?"

Jo wasn't sure what to say, and her ability to speak had disappeared anyway. She'd never truly loved a man before; not until now.

As they held each other and kissed again, Jo realized she didn't have to depend on anyone else. She had proven herself over and over. But Luke's suggestions and insights had been an eye-opener. Maybe she could have more than she ever thought possible, by trusting someone, someone like Luke, to help her realize her dreams and make her wish come true.

As she snuggled deeper into him, she knew this night would stand out in her mind forever. Not only was it the most romantic night she had ever experienced, it was also the night she allowed herself to wish for something more.

"I love you too," she whispered.

CHAPTER 11

The morning dawned with the promise of the sun shining in a gorgeous blue sky above the fresh snow. Their cell service had been restored. They both texted to let everyone know they were okay and would be heading back to the Jeep.

Luke brought the box for the couch into the living area, and with Jo holding the flaps, was able to get it repackaged, then he checked the solar heater and the heat tape in the pump house, confirming the pipes wouldn't freeze. They ate a quick breakfast of hot chocolate and protein bars, and locked up the cabin.

The trip back was even more beautiful with the fresh snow blanketing the ground, making everything look brand new. Jo had a vague idea of how to get back to the Jeep, but was relieved Luke was there and knew the area like his own back-yard. She freed herself from worrying about it, trusting him to lead them home. He found the trail without a problem and showed her the markers that ran along it, barely visible in some areas due to the drifting snow.

They chatted a bit about ideas to get Jo back to Granite Ridge as they walked, and only stopped for a few minutes to drink some water, before plowing ahead. At the parking lot, the jeep was covered in snow, but it didn't take long to dig out and start. The roads hadn't yet been plowed, so the trip back to the lodge was slow and treacherous, but they dropped off her rental gear and made it back to the main lodge before eleven.

Jo went up to her room, while Luke checked in with his supervisor to apologize for his tardiness. First, Jo texted her mom to let her know she was safe and sound, then she took a hot shower, and as soon as she was dressed, dug into her leather bag for a notebook. What Luke had said about goals and steps to get back to Granite Ridge made an impression, and despite thinking there was a slim chance it would work, she was focused on getting her ideas on paper.

While she wrote and sipped a cup of brewed tea, her phone chimed with a text. Luke was going to head home to get cleaned up, and then would be working at the lodge until six o'clock. He invited her to dinner and karaoke when he got off work.

She promised to meet him and bring her list of steps so they could refine them together. Since she'd left home for college, she hadn't had the support of someone by her side, helping her with decisions and plans. She'd always consulted with Maddie, but having Luke's input and knowing he was focused on this with her, only made him more attractive.

She'd been too afraid to say it aloud last night, but had been tempted to add him to the list of things that brought her joy and that she cherished. If she did move back to Granite Ridge, maybe what they had could grow into something more.

Outside of taking a lunch break and nibbling on the snacks Stevie had left in her fridge, Jo worked nonstop on her list of ideas. She spent a ton of time online scouring websites of law firms in the area and looking for office space in Granite Ridge. The cost of living was so much less than it was in Chicago, which buoyed her spirits.

She checked her accounts and made a current list of her assets, so Luke could get an accurate picture. She also outlined the financial goals she had set when she took the job at the law firm.

A knock on the door interrupted her work. She smiled when she saw Stevie standing before her, holding her new dog, Syd, dressed in the cutest little down vest and fur-trimmed hood. His gentle brown eyes looked up at Jo as she held out her arms. "Oh, he's even cuter than the photo you texted me," she said, as she cuddled him. She looked up at her sister. "You should have used your room key."

Stevie's eyebrows rose and she flashed a mischievous grin. "No way, I might walk in and find a hunk of a man in your room. Speaking of handsome men, I hear you got stranded in the storm yesterday and had to spend the night on the mountain with Luke. How was that?" She grinned even wider as she ribbed her sister.

Jo sighed. "Would it surprise you if I told you it was the most romantic time I've ever spent with a man?" She paused and whispered, "I think I love him."

Stevie's eyes widened. "Really? I mean Luke is a great guy, I just can't believe it's so serious between you two. But you've never been one for casual hookups, so maybe I shouldn't be surprised. It's just unexpected."

Jo released Syd, and let him wander around the space, sniffing at the dog bed and scoping out the bag of treats nearby. She opened the package and looked at Stevie for permission.

Stevie nodded as she reached to stroke Syd's silky ears. "I've missed Ed so much, and Syd is the most wonderful gift I could have imagined."

"I'd say he's a special gift from a very thoughtful admirer." The subtle prompt did nothing to elicit more information from her sister.

Stevie's cheeks blushed, and she guided the conversation to a new recipe she wanted to try as she looked to make sure Jo had enough snacks left in her fridge. After, they both sat on the floor and played with Syd, who loved the attention.

Jo gasped when she glanced at her watch. It was almost time to meet Luke. "Sorry, Stevie, I've got to run. Luke and I have dinner plans. You and Syd are welcome to stay as long as you like."

She ran a brush through her hair, added her new poncho over the white sweater she was wearing, and hurried to Jackson's. The hostess led her to a table Luke had reserved, with a good view of the karaoke stage. She ordered a glass of wine and waited, looking over the menu.

Luke came through the door a few minutes later and slipped into the chair next to hers. They were both craving burgers and ordered them with bacon, cheese, and crispy onion strings, along with hand-cut fries. At the last minute, Luke added the pork belly skewers to share as an appetizer.

While they waited, Jo showed him her list and he nodded his head as he studied it, taking a sip from the beer the waitress had delivered. "You've been busy. This is great."

The appetizer arrived as Jo pointed to an item on her list. She couldn't help feeling a hint of excitement at the thought of being able to move back to Granite Ridge. It was like Luke's enthusiasm was contagious. "The easiest thing to do is to ask if the law firm would consider letting me telecommute. That would give me a short-term solution and allow me to move back while I come up with a plan to open my own firm."

"Or," he said, sampling the delicious pork and pineapple flavors smothered in some sort of chili garlic and soy sauce, "take a job at a firm in Boise, which gets you closer, but would give you a gnarly commute if you want to live in Granite Ridge."

She took her first bite. "Wow, these are terrific. Tastes like something Stevie would concoct." She tapped her pen on her notepad. "Right, it's not the best option. I hate to ask to telecommute and then quit. That seems a little sneaky."

"Well, you could tell them you want to move back near your family and are willing to telecommute for three months or six months, whatever you think. That way it seems like you're thinking of them and the workload, giving them time to get used to you being gone."

"I like that idea. I need to take the bar exam here and would have to pay a late fee to take it in February, with the results available in April. If all goes as clockwork, I couldn't open an office until May or June."

"Then we need to see if we can construct a business plan that has you clearing close to the amount you're making in Chicago, taking into account the difference in expenses you'll incur living here." He took another skewer. "I can work on that tomorrow."

Their burgers arrived and they dug into them, talking and going through her notes as they ate. Jo got more excited and more optimistic the more they batted around ideas with Luke suggesting they talk to Mabel and Rusty about the vacant building next to the café. "I know they would make you a deal on the space and would hold it for you until you need it. Gina said it's been empty for months and it's not so large that you'd be paying for wasted square footage."

She jotted the idea on her pad and smiled. "I think this could really work. I'm going to ask Maddie about moving back with her temporarily while I get things figured out. If the telecommuting idea flies, I could put all this in motion right away. If it doesn't, I'm going to have to find a job or stay in Chicago."

"Maybe you could get a telecommuting job with one of the Boise firms?"

She made another note as she finished the last bite of her burger. "That's a good thought."

The sound of "Purple Rain" being sung by a woman in her 50's, whose voice was tinny and off-key filled the air. Jo covered her giggle with her napkin and flashed her eyes at Luke.

He shrugged and said, "I told you nobody is good at karaoke."

He slid from his chair and added their names to the roster, returning with a clever grin.

Jo shook her head and said, "I'm not getting up there in front of all these people."

They watched a few more soloists and then a group sing "YMCA", which got the crowd roaring. Luke leaned across the table and said, "The trick is to pick a song everybody knows."

Luke's name was called and he hurried to the stage and Jo heard the familiar notes from "Sweet Home Alabama" and Luke started singing. He had a good voice and got the crowd involved, urging them to sing and clap.

Jo watched, laughing as he caught her eye several times. When he finished, he was rewarded with cheers and applause, to which he took a bow as he hopped off the stage.

"You were great," said Jo, when he returned to the table. "It must be another one of your little-known abilities, like piano."

"I have many hidden talents," he said, wiggling his eyebrows and leaning closer to kiss her.

After the next song, a horrible but funny rendition of "Dancing Queen" by a group of older women, the disc jockey called Luke and Jo to the stage. Luke grabbed her hand and despite her protests, urged her to the microphone. He showed her the screen with the songs and reminded her to choose one that everyone knew.

Her hands shook as she flipped through the binder of songs the disc jockey held for her. She finally chose "Time of my Life" from one of her favorite movies. Luckily, the duet started with Luke's part and the system was easy to follow, with color coded lyrics for the male and female sections and the parts they sang together.

The audience loved the song and clapped along. Luke even twirled her around a few times while he sang his lines. By the time she reached the middle of the number, Jo's heartbeat had slowed and she wasn't as nervous. Luke was right, when the crowd was involved, there was less pressure on the singer.

They received a standing ovation when they finished and as they left the stage, Luke took her hand in his.

Luke paid for dinner and walked Jo back to the lodge, collecting Finn, and accompanying her upstairs. They lingered over a long kiss at her door, while Finn waited patiently. "Did you have fun tonight?" he asked.

"Once I got over being scared to death, yes." He kissed her again. "Line dancing tomorrow night. Gina's coming with us and wants us to have dinner at the house first and get rid of some leftovers."

Jo bent down and ruffled Finn's ears. "See you tomorrow, sweet boy."

"I'll be home by three o'clock so come early and we'll go over your business plan."

She shut and locked her door, her lips still tingling from his kiss. For the first time in a long time, Jo was excited about change, a chance for a new future, and the idea of seeing Luke beyond the holidays.

CHAPTER 12

J o spent the early morning hours crafting an email to Mr. Gray, the managing partner at her law firm. She thought about it before she went to bed, composing it in her mind, hoping to strike the right balance of gratitude for all she had learned while working there and touting the value of her telecommuting and offering continuity to the projects and clients she worked with, while giving the firm time to replace her.

Luke had taken a rough look at the numbers and assured her the career change wouldn't have a negative impact on her long-term plans and in fact, thought she could add to her bottom line, over time.

Her finger hovered over the button, as she realized when she pressed send, she would be setting things into motion, things she would have a hard time controlling if she had a change of heart. Luke flashed into her mind, as did her sisters and Maddie, and she clicked the button.

As a reward for her bravery, she made a breakfast of left-over wedding cake and tea. As she enjoyed the sugary morsels, she registered for the bar exam, paid the huge late charge, and ordered some study materials. After a shower and getting dressed, she compiled a list of law firms in the Boise area and then checked out attorneys in McCall. Noting there weren't many, she hoped a new office in Granite Ridge might draw clients from all the surrounding areas. She made a list of operating costs for the new office and decided to stop by Rusty's Café just before closing to ask about the space.

Remembering Stevie had left a container of delicious snacks in her fridge, instead of going anywhere for lunch, she nibbled on the bite-sized assortment of pure yumminess. She sent the landlord at her apartment building an email giving notice that she would be out by the end of January. She also let one of the paralegals at work know it would be available and connected her with the landlord, since recently, she had asked about vacancies in the building.

Jo tried to resist the urge to check her email, hoping for a reply from the firm, but couldn't help glancing at it before she gathered her things to head to Granite Ridge.

She hadn't expected a response yet, and when she saw a new email from Mr. Gray, her heart thudded. She sat down on the couch, balancing the laptop on her knees. As she read it, she smiled. He told her how sorry they were to see her go, but understood her desire to be closer to her family. He embraced the idea of having her telecommute for as long as she wanted, even offering an indefinite timeframe. The firm would pay to fly her back to Chicago if they needed any face-to-face meetings and were thrilled she was willing to stay on in any capacity. He also offered to help her find a new position in the Boise area and mentioned firms where he had contacts.

She tapped her feet on the floor and flung her arms in the air. The first step, the hardest, had been a success and would mean she wouldn't have to rush to open an office, but could take her time. Now, she had to tackle the email she dreaded most – the one to Love Links. After several drafts, she finally hit the send button and shut her eyes thinking of Nina, the president, and all the other board members she admired. She told them how much the organization meant to her and that she hoped to start something similar in her hometown. Tears stung as she thought of the kids she would miss and the upcoming graduations she wouldn't attend.

She checked that item off the list and smiled when she read the next one. She knew Maddie would let her stay at the house until she could find a place, but also didn't want to assume anything after their conversation the other day and Maddie's thoughts about downsizing.

She glanced at her watch and texted her mom to see if she had time for a quick chat. Maddie called back immediately and said she was out of the lodge enjoying snowmobiling, but could talk on the phone and wondered what Jo needed.

Jo smiled, glad that her mom was having fun. She took a deep breath and tried to curb her enthusiasm when she explained her desire to move back to Granite Ridge and that she would be telecommuting until she could swing opening her own firm. As Maddie asked a few questions, Jo told her Luke had inspired the idea and encouraged her. "I was hoping you'd let me move home with you until I can get organized and find a place."

Maddie squealed with delight. "Of course, that would be wonderful. Oh, I've wished something like this for you for so long, Jo. I'm so happy and over the moon that you and Luke have become so close."

Maddie rambled on about how wonderful it would be to have her home again, close to everyone and all the fun they could have. The connection began to deteriorate and they disconnected, promising to talk more later.

With a spring in her step, Jo packed her laptop into the leather satchel and hurried downstairs. She made it to town with only a few minutes to spare and walked through the door of Rusty's Café to find Mabel and Rusty sitting at the counter enjoying a cup of coffee and a slice of pie.

"Jo, come on in, sweetie," said Mabel. "We were just fixing to close for the day. Can I get you something?"

She shook her head and slipped onto the stool next to her. "No, I was just hoping to talk to you for a few minutes about the vacant space next door." She explained about her plans to move back and a future law firm, which was at least six months down the road.

Like Maddie, they were both overjoyed at the thought of her living in Granite Ridge and loved the idea of having her next door. Rusty stood and put his hands on her shoulders. "We'll make you a deal you can't refuse. It's been sitting empty and we'd love to have it filled and active, so let's just say we'll make the rent as low as it needs to be to make it work for you, dear."

"It would be wonderful to have an attorney in town. Everyone has to go down to Boise if they need anything."

Jo nodded and said, "That's what I was thinking. Luke and I are working on a business plan and thought I could fill a need in the area."

Rusty laughed and said, "I think Luke might be working on more than just a business plan."

Mabel poked him with her elbow. "He just means Luke is more upbeat and has a permanent grin on his face since you've arrived. He's in here every morning on his way to work and I daresay he mentions you more than anyone. I think the boy is smitten."

Jo blushed and put her arm around Mabel. "The feeling is mutual. He's as kind as I remember and I just love being with him. He makes me happy. Happier than I've ever been."

She couldn't get out the door without a box of pie slices. She promised to keep them informed of her plans and hugged them both goodbye.

Luke and Finn were home when she arrived. After greeting her with a lovely kiss, Luke motioned her through the house and back to his den, where he was working on the computer. She shared the good news about the office space and the telecommuting. He held her in a long embrace and kissed the top of her head. "Oh, that is great news. This was all meant to be."

He showed her the business plan and the financial projections he had worked on for her personal finances as well as those of her new firm. After they reviewed it, Jo began to understand that the shift could mean she would reach her personal financial goals even quicker than she planned.

He dug out the binder with his own business plan and said, "You've inspired me. I've got an appointment with Mr. Jeffries right after the first of the year and I'm going to make this a reality."

"Well, if you need an office in town, I'm sure there's room in the new office space next to the café. What could be more fitting for Granite Ridge than an attorney and outdoor adventure service all under one roof?"

He chuckled. "Sounds good to me. It actually would be a good idea to have a presence in town and at the lodge." He checked his watch and added, "I better get dinner reheated, so we can eat as soon as Gina gets home and get out to the lodge for the big dance."

After four hours of nonstop line dancing, Jo had scooted her boogie until it wouldn't move. She was exhausted, but had never had so much fun. Gina was hilarious and like Luke, a great dancer. She and Luke teased each other mercilessly, both of them possessing a great sense of humor with a healthy dose of sarcasm they weren't afraid to unleash.

Having finished one more glass of wine after their last dance, Jo insisted she could find her own way back to her room, with Luke leaving her at the door of the main lodge. She didn't want Gina to have to wait in his truck any longer than necessary. He hugged Jo close to him and covered her mouth with his. As their kiss intensified, Jo's knees weakened. She wobbled and he caught her, laughing. "I think you're the first girl I've literally swept off her feet."

She met his playful eyes. "Thank you, Luke."

He steadied her and said, "Of course. You're still okay to get to your room?"

She nodded. "I mean, thank you for everything. For making me step out of my comfort zone, for helping me figure out how to make my wish a reality. For all of it. I love you so very much."

He kissed her again and smiled. "I love you more."

Jo spent the next two days soaking in the relaxing hot tubs on the huge deck behind the lodge, with a stunning view of the mountain slopes, recovering from both the snowshoeing and marathon dance party.

She received a lovely and heartfelt reply from Nina and several of the other board members at Love Links. They all offered their expertise, influence, and even money to help her start a local Love Links program in Granite Ridge. They also suggested she continue mentoring a few of her clients, via video chats, and get them through the school year. No one knew more than Jo, how fragile connections could be for foster children, and she hated the idea of leaving them. She gladly agreed to the idea and her mind began to spin with plans for getting a non-profit set up in Idaho.

In between soaks, emails with coworkers, researching movers, and perusing housing in Granite Falls, she attended one of the paint and sip sessions at the lodge. Ever since meeting Gina and having her be so welcoming, she wanted to do something special for her. When she saw the easel with the pretty snow-covered tree strung with lights, she knew it would make the perfect gift for her.

She called Doris and was able to chat with her for almost an hour. She sounded cheery and in good spirits, having resolved herself to moving to Texas. She and her husband had lived in that Chicago apartment for years and part of the reason she hadn't moved sooner was because of him. She felt connected to him there and didn't want to lose that. With the fall and surgery, reality had set in and she realized she needed to be with her family, where she'd have a support system.

Jo broke the news to her and told her she was also going to be moving back to Idaho and how happy it made her. She teased her and told Doris there was no point in staying in Chicago if Doris was moving to Texas. They laughed and chatted, like they always did. Jo's voice cracked when she told her how much she would miss her and she hoped she would be able to visit her in Texas.

She had just dried her eyes after hanging up from her call with Doris, when Luke texted and invited her to a late breakfast downstairs. She had time to join him before her appointment for a manicure to get her nails done for the New Year's Eve party. They met at the restaurant and she filled him in on her progress with organizing her move back to Granite Falls. "I'm trying to decide if it's worth moving my stuff or if I should just sell it. I don't have that much and finding a mover is a nightmare, not to mention super expensive."

"I could take a few days off, come back with you and get a rental truck and drive home with you."

Her nose wrinkled. "You'd really do that? That's a real pain."

"I love a good road trip. What's more fun that driving across the country in the dead of winter? What could go wrong?" He referenced *Planes, Trains, and Automobiles*, laughed and reached for his coffee. "Seriously, it will be a piece of cake. Trust me I've done worse."

"If you're sure, that would be terrific. I'll look into rentals. I have to be out of my apartment by the end of January, but it can be earlier." Her eyes widened, "There's another thing I need to do. Buy a car. I don't need one in the city, but living here, it's not optional, plus I'll need one that can handle snow."

"Dad has a ton of contacts for vehicles. I'll get him working on that when he gets home next week." Luke finished his last bite of omelet. "When do you fly back to Chicago?"

"I leave on the second."

"Do you have a date in mind to get back here?"

"Nothing firm. It won't take long to pack the apartment. It's small. Work is pretty flexible; I'll just need a couple of days to work out the details of the telecommuting agreement and then could be ready to go."

"Maybe I should just fly back with you and we can just bang it out and get back here within a week?"

Jo couldn't believe her life had changed so quickly. When she had boarded the plane for Boise, she tried not to think about how sad she would be to leave and now, she'd never have to feel that way again. She'd be there for Maddie and Nan, be able to celebrate with Hailey and see her much more often, and see Stevie in person for their marathon chats, instead of on the tiny screen of her phone. Alissa and Jed wouldn't be far away and she suspected they'd be spending all the important holidays in Granite Ridge. She knew she had made the right decision and when she looked into Luke's eyes, she was even more convinced.

Her wish to move home had never included having a man like Luke in her life. It was more than she ever would have dreamed possible. To think she hadn't even thought about him until she saw him outside the lodge. By chance, Finn reintroduced them. Maybe it wasn't by chance. Whatever had worked to bring them back together, she was grateful.

Without Luke, she would have never been brave enough to consider deviating from her plan and looking at possibilities.

The thought of not having to get on a plane alone filled her with joy. "That would be wonderful, if you can swing it."

"Consider it done. I just need to book a flight."

"I'll do it, just text me your full name on your ID and your date of birth and I'll get you on the same flight."

He pulled out his phone and seconds later hers chimed. "Done." He winked and said, "I hate to eat and run, but need to get back to work. I offered to work the late shift tonight to make up for our little snowshoeing adventure, so I won't see you until tomorrow." He slid out of the booth and came around to her side, kissing her. "I'll pick you up in your room for the party, okay?"

She nodded. "I'll be ready. I'll pop down for a coffee tonight and say hello."

After he left, she poured another cup of tea from the pot and used her app to book him on her flight. She keyed in his information, happily using a chunk of her frequent flyer miles to get him in first class and sent him a confirmation.

He replied with a happy face, a kiss, and a heart.

CHAPTER 13

J o packed most of her clothes, leaving out only what she needed for tomorrow and the plane trip back to Chicago. She had reserved a rental truck for the move and had everything as coordinated as possible. She was looking forward to spending time with Luke in the city, showing him some of the sites.

She dressed in the long black velvet skirt she had purchased and added the pretty green blouse. Maddie had let her borrow a set of emerald earrings that went with the necklace she had given her. When she was having her manicure yesterday, she made an appointment to have her hair done in another updo, like she had for the wedding. No matter how hard she tried or how many videos she watched online, she couldn't get her hair to do what the stylist had done.

She admired her hair in the mirror and once dressed, agreed with the manicurist who had insisted she add a delicate sprinkling of glitter across the ends of Jo's clear nails. The woman assured Jo they looked festive, but classy, and Jo agreed.

She wore the open toe sandals she had packed and added the furry wrap she had worn to the wedding. She gave herself the once over in the full-length mirror and smiled. The outfit was perfect for the party and more than that, she glowed with happiness. Jo never thought of herself as attractive, but looking at her reflection now, she looked different than usual and she knew it was because of the joy she felt inside. If being in love made her look like this, she should have tried it years ago.

A soft knock on her door interrupted her musings. She hurried to it and found Luke grinning. Her breath caught at the sight of him in a black tuxedo with an emerald green pocket square that matched her blouse. "Wow," she said, "you look amazing."

He presented her with one red rose and came through the door. "You get more beautiful every time I see you."

He wandered into the suite and stood by the fireplace.

She asked him to put her room key in his pocket, since she wasn't taking a purse. "Are you ready?" She tilted her head toward the door.

"Can I ask you something?" he said, slipping his hand in his pocket.

"Sure," she smiled and gave him a questioning look.

He took her hand in his and bent down in front of her, slipping the blue velvet box from his pocket. "I can think of no better way to end this year and begin a new one than with asking you to be my wife, my forever, my best friend. Over these two weeks, I've realized I don't want a world without you in it. I love you and I can't get you out of my mind. I found what I've been missing in my life and it's you." He flipped open the box to reveal a dazzling princess cut diamond ring.

Jo's wrap fell to the ground as she covered her mouth with her hand and gasped. "Oh, my, that is gorgeous." She moved her eyes between the ring and his expectant gaze. She knew she should think through such a big decision, but in her heart, she realized she had found her forever." She bobbed her head and bent to kiss him. "Yes, yes, yes."

He stood and lifted her off the ground, twirling her around as he kissed her. "You had me going there for a minute." He put her down and slipped the ring on her finger.

She held it out in front of her, admiring the sparkle. "You've made the happiest week of my life even better. I love you more than you will ever know."

His face was smeared with the lipstick Maddie had loaned her and she dragged him into the bathroom and helped him wipe it off, while she attempted to fix her own face.

"Do you know how excited Mom and everyone is going to be?" She watched him in the mirror as she dabbed at her lips.

"Well, like a proper gentleman, I asked Maddie for her permission, so she knows. To say she was excited, would be a vast understatement. She could hardly contain herself, but I made her promise to keep it a secret. We can tell everyone tonight."

He placed the wrap around her shoulders, kissed her carefully, so as not to mess up her lipstick and slipped her arm through his. They checked in at the welcome desk and found the table Maddie had reserved, but all the chairs were empty. The ceiling was dripping with white twinkly lights and the dance floor was already full. A huge buffet lined one wall and the savory aroma made Jo hungry.

After dragging Luke to the buffet line, they danced several dances under the shimmering mirrored balls installed in the ceiling. Amid all the revelers, she caught up with Hailey and confirmed that the sisters and Maddie were to meet up on the patio for their traditional toast at midnight.

The elegant dresses worn by most of the women and the tuxedo-clad men dancing to the sultry jazz music made it seem like they were all there to celebrate Jo and Luke's news. She had never felt such joy and excitement and couldn't wait to show her sisters her gorgeous ring that glimmered each time it caught the lights from above.

They danced until the last minute, when they nabbed two flutes of champagne from the table and hurried to the patio, just in time to hear the beginning of the countdown to midnight. Jo admired the shimmering lights in the shrubbery surrounding the patio and the larger globe lights strung across the entire area, making a glowing canopy above. Looking beyond she could see the stars littered across the sky and the dark, imposing mountain peaks that were always there, like sentinels, high above Granite Ridge.

She took in the happy smiles on the faces of her sisters, Maddie, and Nan. It had been an incredible couple of weeks, full of surprises. Ever since they had lived with Maddie, they had celebrated with a toast and shared a wish or a goal for the new year. She remembered that first year, all of them holding their beautiful flutes of sparkling apple juice, but over time they had advanced to champagne. Just like that first celebration, as the clock struck twelve, they raised their glasses amid cries of "Happy New Year."

When it was her turn to toast, Jo raised her glass, and looked into the eyes of the man she loved smiling back at her before meeting her mother's knowing grin. "Tonight, Luke surprised me with a lovely proposal and I said yes."

Her sisters squealed and she held up her hand. "And, I'm moving back to Granite Ridge to open my own law firm and be closer to all of you."

Cheers erupted from the group and each of her sisters rushed to gawk at the ring on her finger. Jed clapped Luke on the shoulder and Maddie swooped in and hugged him in a long embrace. Tears glistened in Nan's eyes as she kissed Jo's cheek.

After the excitement and more congratulatory hugs and kisses from her sisters, Luke took Jo's hand and they circled the dance floor for their first dance of the new year, their arms wrapped around each other as they swayed to the music. They kissed as the song ended, Jo knowing it was going to be her happiest year yet and that no matter how old she gets, she'll never underestimate the power of Christmas wishes – the proof of them coming true standing next to her, in the man she loved and knew would be her forever.

EPILOGUE

JO INVITES YOU TO CONTINUE THE SERIES

J o is still amazed at how much her life changed over the past couple of weeks. She expected the holidays to be different, with the wedding drama, but she never imagined a vacation in the snow-covered mountains and an encounter with a friendly golden retriever would set her on a path that would forever change her life.

Now that you know what has happened to Jo over the last fifteen years and experienced the magic of *Christmas Wishes*, she wants to make sure you learn all about what happened to her soul sisters, including her mom, in their own stories. You're in for a treat and a few more surprises as you read each one of the books in the series!

Don't miss the other books in SOUL SISTERS AT CEDAR MOUNTAIN LODGE and you can read a sneak preview of the next book in the series, *Christmas Hope*, on the following pages.

Book 1: Christmas Sisters – FREE prologue book
Book 2: Christmas Kisses by Judith Keim
Book 3: Christmas Wishes by Tammy L. Grace
Book 4: Christmas Hope by Violet Howe
Book 5: Christmas Dreams by Ev Bishop
Book 6: Christmas Rings by Tess Thompson

CONTINUE THE STORY

CHRISTMAS HOPE BY VIOLET HOWE
CHAPTER 1

"Snow's getting heavier," Claire said as she leaned forward to look up through the windshield. "I hope we're able to make it to the lodge before the road becomes impassable."

Maddie shot a glare at her mother but managed to bite back an irritated response.

After all, Claire hadn't caused the storm in the east that had delayed her incoming flight, so it wasn't fair to be upset with her. Of course, if Claire hadn't booked a Caribbean cruise so close to Alissa's wedding date, then there wouldn't have been a need for flights at all. Claire would have been home, and they could have left earlier in the day and already been at the lodge with everyone else.

Maddie tightened her grip on the steering wheel, frustrated at the delay in getting to Alissa so she could see for herself that her daughter was okay.

It still didn't seem real that the wedding was off. How could Jed have done this to Alissa? How could he cancel their wedding mere days before they were to say their vows?

Maddie knew Jed loved her daughter. It was evident to anyone who saw them together. She'd heard it in his voice when he spoke about Alissa and seen it in his eyes every time he looked at her. They'd truly seemed like a strong match with a bright future.

What on earth had brought it all crashing down?

That family of his was likely the cause. Alissa had never felt accepted by them, even though Jed had assured her that all was well, and it was just their manner to be standoffish. His mother, in particular, had been a thorn in Alissa's side, but the woman's passive-aggressive tactics had made it hard for Alissa to make a case with Jed.

The two of them rarely argued, but when they did, it usually pertained to his mother. Maddie had been hesitant to get involved or to weigh in too heavily, but she had, on occasion, tried to gingerly express her concerns to Jed. Unfortunately, he was too blinded by love in both directions to see the situation clearly. He believed the two most important women in his life would get along fine once they realized how much he loved them both.

In the past few months, it had looked as though he might be right. As the wedding date drew closer, his parents had arranged a rehearsal dinner at the lodge for the night before the wedding, although Maddie had suspected it was more about appearances than any genuine enthusiasm for Jed and Alissa's union.

So, if it wasn't his family, then what? What had made Jed back out? Was it cold feet? Was he having doubts?

Maddie wished she could talk to him and find out. She also wished she could wring his neck and throw him off the edge of the Grand Canyon, but she'd promised Alissa she wouldn't do either of those things.

Her heart hurt to think of what Alissa must be feeling. Though they'd texted and spoken several times on the phone, that wasn't the same as talking face to face. Maddie knew she wouldn't be able to relax until she could get to the lodge and wrap her arms around her daughter. She needed to be there to comfort Alissa and make sure she was okay, but the weather seemed determined to thwart her mission, first with the airport delays and now with the drive to the lodge taking longer than it should have.

Alissa was already surrounded by love, of course. Despite the canceled plans, all the sisters had made their way to the lodge without hesitation to show their support and help her through one of the hardest weeks of her life.

A warm pride swelled in Maddie's chest, and she couldn't help but smile. Each of her girls might have come to her alone fifteen years ago, but since that first fateful Christmas, they'd been a true family, supporting each other through good times and bad. The bond the girls shared had been forged in the heart, as strong and unbreakable as any blood tie ever could have been.

"Did I tell you Royce won the ship's dance contest for men over seventy?" Claire asked.

Maddie suppressed a groan. The last thing she wanted to hear was another Royce story. Her mother had talked incessantly about the man nonstop ever since Maddie picked her up at the airport.

Actually, it went back farther than that. Royce Campbell had been an ever-present topic of conversation since he'd asked Claire to join him on the floor at the senior living center's swing dance class six months earlier. Her mother had been completely smitten, but Maddie was not a fan.

In theory, Maddie had no problem with Claire dating. She wanted her mother to be happy, and she certainly didn't begrudge her the pursuit of love and companionship. Though Claire was a natural social butterfly who kept herself busy with a myriad of activities and social engagements, she'd never been romantically linked with anyone in the years since Maddie's father had died.

In fact, Claire had never shown the slightest interest in dating before she met Royce, but she had certainly made up for lost time. At first, Maddie was amused by her mother's sudden doe-eyed giddiness, but as the geriatric couple's relationship blossomed and their physical affection began to resemble that of hormonal teenagers, it had been harder for Maddie to maintain her enthusiasm.

Perhaps she could have accepted it better if Royce were less, well, *Royce*. He had a gregarious personality that bordered on obnoxious. He had aged well and was handsome enough, but the confidence he exuded and the charm he oozed was too over-the-top for Maddie's liking. For the life of her, she couldn't understand how her normally down-to-earth, level-headed mother could possibly be attracted to someone who came across like a snake oil salesman peddling love potion.

In a matter of weeks, the two had become almost inseparable, and though Maddie had realized on some level that it seemed to be getting more serious, she was still stunned when Claire announced they were taking a seven-day cruise together to celebrate the holidays.

"What? But you've been terrified of water your entire life," Maddie had protested. "You've never been on a boat. You don't even know how to swim, Mom."

"I don't need to know how to swim to take a cruise, Madeline, and it's a *ship*, not a boat. Royce says you can't even feel it moving. He says it's like being on a big city floating out at sea. They even have trees and a park with artificial grass on one of the decks."

"It's still surrounded by water. What if you need to evacuate?"

Claire had sighed and brushed away Maddie's concerns with a flip of her hand. "Don't be so dramatic, dear. Royce says the chances of an emergency are very slim when you look at the overall number of people cruising every day. Besides, they'll supply life jackets if there is an emergency, so I'll just float. I won't need to swim."

Maddie had looked at her mother as though she'd

sprouted an extra head. Where was the practical, logical thinker who had raised Maddie? What had this man done to her mother's common sense?

"A seven-day cruise seems really long," Maddie had said, trying a different tactic. "What if you don't like it? What if you get seasick? What if you don't like being around Royce as much as you think you might? Seven days with someone is a lot to take on."

Especially Royce.

Maddie couldn't stand to be around him for more than an hour. "You guys haven't known each other that long. Don't you think it might be too soon for such an extended trip?"

Claire had smiled with a patronizing expression. "Sweetheart, we're both in our seventies. We don't have the luxury of time. We've been granted a second chance at happiness, and we intend to grab it by the horns and enjoy every single minute we have together."

Maddie had caught herself secretly hoping something would happen to make them cancel the trip. Nothing tragic or devastating, of course. Maybe a weather situation. Or a bad case of hemorrhoids to prevent Royce from traveling.

She'd admonished herself for being selfish, and she'd even managed to put on a happy face when she dropped Claire off at the airport a week ago, but it was harder to pretend she was interested in hearing all the details of the cruise when her sole focus was making her way to the top of the mountain where Alissa sat waiting with her heart shattered.

If Claire noticed a lack of enthusiasm from her daughter, she never let on.

"You should have seen him," Claire said with a girlish giggle when she'd finished recalling Royce's prowess on the cruise ship dance floor. "It was like John Travolta had been reincarnated."

"John Travolta is still very much alive, Mom," Maddie

said as she reached to turn the defroster up higher. "And younger than Royce by quite a few years."

"Not that many years. I'd say Travolta has to be nearing seventy, wouldn't you think?"

They'd just entered one of the worst of the curves in the narrow mountain road, and despite Maddie slowing down, the car began to slide. She let off the accelerator and turned the wheel into the slide to counteract it.

"Careful," Claire said after a sharp intake of breath. "These roads can be awfully treacherous in a heavy snow. We should have stayed at home tonight and struck out in the morning once the plows had—oh my goodness! Look! There!"

Want to continue on Maddie's journey with her? Download Christmas Hope at www.books2read.com/ChristmasHope and find it at your favorite online vendor!

ACKNOWLEDGMENTS

The idea for this series sprouted from a dinner conversation with my author friends during a conference we attended in 2019. We thought it would be fun to write a connected series and loved the idea of using sisters of the heart, or soul sisters as our theme. After some quick brainstorming, our story took shape and then we went home to craft our characters.

This project has been full of fun and also challenges to make sure our stories meshed. I love my character, Jo, and had so much fun creating her story. While we each worked on our own story, much like the characters we created, I felt we all became soul sisters ourselves.

My thanks to my editor, Angela, for finding my mistakes and helping me polish *Christmas Wishes*. I also owe a debt of gratitude to my author friends: Ev Bishop, Violet Howe, Judy Keim, and Tess Thompson. We've planned our releases so that readers will get the next installment in the series only one week apart during the initial release period. Although centered around the holidays, the stories are meant to serve up warm wishes to you, regardless of the season in which you're reading them.

I hope you enjoyed Christmas Wishes and in case you've only read my book in the series, be sure to pick up *Christmas Sisters* (Book 1), the prologue novella where you'll meet all the characters, and check out Hailey's story in *Christmas Kisses*, Book 2. To meet the authors of the series, learn fun character insights, and more, be sure to join our Facebook Group, Soul Sisters Chat here: https://www.facebook.com/groups/soulsistersbookchat

I so appreciate all of the readers who have taken the time to provide reviews of my books. These reviews are especially important in promoting future books, so if you enjoy my novels, please consider leaving a review. Just visit my author page on the major book retailers' sites and select a book to leave your review. I also encourage you to follow me on book retailers and BookBub, where leaving a review is even easier and you'll be the first to know about new releases and deals.

Remember to visit my website at http://www.tammylgrace.com and join my mailing list for my exclusive group of readers. I've also got a fun Book Buddies Facebook Group. That's the best place to find me and get a chance to participate in my giveaways. Join my Facebook group at https://www.facebook.com/groups/AuthorTammyLGraceBookBuddies/ and keep in touch—I'd love to hear from you.

With warm Christmas wishes,

Tammy

FROM THE AUTHOR

Thank you for reading CHRISTMAS WISHES. Don't miss any of the SOUL SISTERS AT CEDAR MOUNTAIN LODGE BOOKS. Links to all of them are provided in the next pages. You can also get a sneak peek at CHRISTMAS HOPE, BOOK 4 in the series, at the end of this book.

If you enjoy holiday stories, be sure and check out my CHRISTMAS IN SILVER FALLS SERIES and CHRISTMAS IN SNOW VALLEY. They are small-town Christmas stories of hope, friendship, and family. If you're a new reader and enjoy women's fiction, you'll want to try my HOMETOWN HARBOR SERIES, filled with the complex relationships of friendship and family. Set in the picturesque San Juan Islands in Washington, you'll escape with a close-knit group of friends and their interwoven lives filled with both challenges and joys. Each book in the series focuses on a different woman and her journey of self-discovery. Be sure and download the free novella, HOMETOWN HARBOR: THE BEGINNING. It's a prequel to FINDING HOME that I know you'll enjoy.

For mystery lovers, I write a series that features a lovable private detective, Coop, and his faithful golden retriever, Gus.

If you like whodunits that will keep you guessing until the end, you'll enjoy the COOPER HARRINGTON DETECTIVE NOVELS.

The first book, BEACH HAVEN, in my new GLASS BEACH COTTAGE SERIES is also loved by readers. It is a heartwarming story of a woman's resilience buoyed by the bonds of friendship, an unexpected gift, and the joy she finds in helping others. As with all my books, the furry four-legged characters play a prominent role.

The two books I've written as Casey Wilson, A DOG'S HOPE and A DOG'S CHANCE have received enthusiastic support from my readers and if you're a dog-lover, are must-reads.

I'd love to send you my exclusive interview with the canine companions in the Hometown Harbor Series as a thank-you for joining my exclusive group of readers. You can sign up www.tammylgrace.com by clicking this link: https://wp.me/P9umIy-e

MORE BOOKS BY TAMMY L. GRACE

Don't miss the other books in **SOUL SISTERS AT CEDAR MOUNTAIN LODGE** and you can read a sneak preview of the next book in the series, *Christmas Hope*, on the preceding pages.

Book 1: Christmas Sisters – FREE prologue book
Book 2: Christmas Kisses by Judith Keim
Book 3: Christmas Wishes by Tammy L. Grace
Book 4: Christmas Hope by Violet Howe
Book 5: Christmas Dreams by Ev Bishop
Book 6: Christmas Rings by Tess Thompson

COOPER HARRINGTON DETECTIVE NOVELS

Killer Music
Deadly Connection
Dead Wrong

HOMETOWN HARBOR SERIES

Hometown Harbor: The Beginning (FREE Prequel Novella)
Finding Home
Home Blooms
A Promise of Home
Pieces of Home
Finally Home
Forever Home

CHRISTMAS NOVELLAS

A Season for Hope: Christmas in Silver Falls Book 1
The Magic of the Season: Christmas in Silver Falls Book 2

Christmas in Snow Valley: A Hometown Christmas Novella

GLASS BEACH COTTAGE SERIES

Beach Haven

WRITING AS CASEY WILSON

A Dog's Hope
A Dog's Chance

Remember to subscribe to Tammy's exclusive group of readers for your gift, only available to readers on her mailing list. Sign up at www.tammylgrace.com. Follow this link to subscribe at https://wp.me/P9umIy-e and you'll receive the exclusive interview she did with all the canine characters in her Hometown Harbor Series.

Follow Tammy on Facebook by liking her author page. You may also follow Tammy on Amazon or at BookBub by clicking on the follow button.

ABOUT THE AUTHOR

Tammy L. Grace is the *USA Today* bestselling and award-winning author of the Cooper Harrington Detective Novels, the best-selling Hometown Harbor Series, and the Glass Beach Cottage Series, along with several sweet Christmas novellas. Tammy also writes under the pen name of Casey Wilson for Bookouture. You'll find Tammy online at www.tammylgrace.com where you can join her mailing list and be part of her exclusive group of readers. Connect with Tammy on social media by clicking on the icons below.

facebook.com/tammylgrace.books

twitter.com/TammyLGrace

instagram.com/authortammylgrace

bookbub.com/authors/tammy-l-grace

goodreads.com/tammylgrace

pinterest.com/tammylgrace

amazon.com/author/tammylgrace

Made in United States
North Haven, CT
17 August 2023